A Rachel Markham Mystery

THE RIVERTON CASE

BOOK 3 - IN THE MYSTERY SERIES

notionpress.com

A Rachel Markham Mystery

THE RIVERTON CASE
BOOK 3 - IN THE MYSTERY SERIES

P.B. KOLLERI

notionpress.com

Notion Press

First published by NotionPress 2013

Copyright © P.B Kolleri 2013

All Rights Reserved.

ISBN: 978-14-92939-91-7

Dedicated to the life & times of a beautiful Indian Princess
And the extraordinary life she led

Her Royal Highness Maharani Brinda Devi
of Kapurthala State

The Voyage to India.
September 1947.

Twilight was about to set in as the regal RMS Arundel sluiced through the choppy waters of the dreaded Bay of Biscay. Rachel stood upon the aft deck, high above the ship's stern, holding on to the rails tightly. Despite the heaving and rolling motion, which had sent many able bodied passengers including Jeremy straight to the cabins, Rachel stood feeling free and in a way, powerful, as if the icy wind that whipped her cloak about her, lent her its wings. She was mesmerized by the changing colour of the sky mirrored by the moving sea and the steady V-shaped pattern of foam left in the ship's wake. She found herself thinking, 'This is beauty in motion – sheer and intense, the kind of beauty that can drive one mad or worse, make a poet out of one.' The thought made her smile. 'I don't suppose there are many poets aboard, though.'

They had set sail in the morning from Southampton, the day before and the ship was practically empty on the way out. So far, Rachel had only seen a scattering of British ICS (Indian Civil Service) men and several well-to-do Indian passengers. More passengers were expected to come aboard in Marseilles, including His Highness - the Prince of Dharanpore along with his entourage. Most people preferred to travel over land to Marseilles, to avoid sailing through the unpredictable and usually vicious weather that rocked boats through the Bay of Biscay, this time of the year. Rachel wouldn't hear of it, when Jeremy suggested they could do the same. She wanted to experience it all. 'Where's your sense of adventure, darling?'

At the moment, Jeremy was back in his cabin cursing his wife's sense of adventure. Despite the Captain's brisk and cheerful assurance upon boarding the vessel that they had heavy duty ship stabilizers on board, RMS Arundel was currently being tossed about like the proverbial cork on the sea. Needless to say, this had the amusing affect of sending both Colonel Riverton and Jeremy Richards to their cabins, in record time, looking rather green around the gills. Adding insult to injury, to Jeremy's immense chagrin, Rachel seemed to be handling it rather well, to the point of enjoying herself. She tucked him in and then told him breezily, as he lay groaning on his bunk with sea sickness that she was going to go back up on the deck for some 'refreshing sea air'.

Rachel had been awestruck by the sheer size and beauty of RMS Arundel at anchor. She soon found out that it was a 686 feet long steamship that boasted a speed of 20 knots and could contain close to twelve hundred souls on board. The ship had been authorized to carry Royal mail consignments hence its RMS status. During the war, she had been pressed into war service and carried troups and ammunition across the seas. Only recently, the ocean liner had been refurbished to its former glory by The Army and Navy Stores and was now on its maiden civilian voyage. The first class decks included a 'social' room for various social dances and events, which was the size of a large ball room, a card room, a smoking room with a well appointed bar, a heated swimming pool, a billiards room, a well stocked library and two massive dining halls, apart from luxurious sun decks to amble about on. Half the cabins in the massive ship's upper deck had been booked for His Highness, the Prince of Dharanpore, his family and their travelling companions as they headed home to their Indian Palace, after their annual sojourn of six months in Europe's finest hotspots.

Rachel and Jeremy's trip to India had been sponsored by the Royal family of Dharanpore, in an effort to get to the bottom of a puzzling and yet to be solved case that had occurred two years ago in 1945. Colonel Riverton's daughter – Kitty Riverton had been murdered in the Dharanpore Palace and the priceless necklace she had worn on the night of the murder, which was encrusted with a massive 27 carat star ruby called the 'Pride of Dharanpore' had gone missing. The young Prince, who had lent Kitty the necklace, on his part felt responsible for her murder and the loss of a valuable royal jewel and wanted no stone unturned to catch the culprit and recover the stone. To that end, he and his father,

Maharajah Paramjit Dharan had requested Colonel Riverton to make his way to London from India and hire the best possible professional detectives in England.

Colonel Riverton had met up with an old school friend of his - Chief Inspector Harrow of Scotland Yard, who had spoken highly of Rachel's detecting abilities and asked the Colonel to meet both Rachel and Jeremy. After his initial meeting with the duo at The Savoy, Colonel Riverton had shared his reservations around hiring the detective duo with the Chief Inspector. 'I can't believe that this little chit of a girl is the best detective you can come up with!' Harrow had then made a good natured bet with him, 'Don't go by appearances, old boy! I'll eat my hat if this little chit of a girl doesn't solve your case. She's already solved two baffling cases that I am ashamed to admit, had my police force going about in circles, that too within the span of a year. I wouldn't underestimate her, if I were you. Plus don't forget, if you can persuade her to go to India, you also get the added benefit of having one of my most experienced men – Jeremy Richards, on board. I'd give anything to have him back on the force.'

After some debate, the Colonel had acquiesced, grumbling, 'I'll have a hell of a time trying to convince the Maharajah, though.' As it turned out, the Maharajah, who had spent the past six months in Europe, did not need convincing. He had already read about the high profile cases at Rutherford Hall and Ravenrock House, which had been plastered all over the Continental newspapers. The upshot was that within a fortnight, Jeremy and Rachel were accompanying Riverton to India.

Since they were now on their way to India on the Maharajah's express invitation, they had been allocated a first class cabin on the upper deck on the starboard side, which was considered the fashionable side. 'You're on the same side as the ship's Captain and His Highness - the Prince Ravindra Richard', Colonel Riverton had hastened to inform them. While their cabin was in no way as spacious as Colonel Riverton's, it was as tastefully decorated as his, with beautiful soft furnishing and elegant fittings. And Rachel had playfully told Jeremy as they settled in, 'At least we get to travel in style, even if we do occasionally bump our heads getting out of bed.'

The near empty status of the India bound ship was easily explained. Everyone knew that India had achieved her hard won freedom from 200 years of British Raj, in a momentous celebration of human spirit on the 15th of August, a mere fortnight ago. Jeremy and Rachel had sat side by side, near the fireplace at Sunny Ridge and heard Jawaharlal Nehru's moving speech, 'A Tryst with Destiny', as it was broadcast over the wireless to the rest of the world. Colonel Riverton had explained that RMS Arundel would be packed like a tin of sardines on her return journey, as many British ICS officers and their families, who had stayed back in order to facilitate the smooth transition of power through Indian Independence, would now be ready to make their way back home from Indian shores. Though 'home', he had gone on to explain, would be a strange land for most of these ICS men and their families, especially the ones who had lived in, and loved India for three generations or more.

Rachel had ventured, 'But surely, they will be pleased to be back on British soil, to be reunited with their relations, familiar faces and places?'

'You'd think most people would *want* to raise their families away from diseases, and the infernal heat and dust of India, and so on, eh?' Colonel Riverton added, with a knowing smile.

'I suppose so, yes. Not to mention the poverty and communal violence - I hear it's getting worse every day.'

Colonel Riverton responded with a shake of his head and a chuckle, 'All these assumptions are based upon irrefutable logic, my dear, but ask anyone of these men and they will tell you that there is another side to India, where no amount of logic works - the heart of India, that casts a spell on you – one that's hard to break. Once you're there, you'll see.'

Rachel wanted to see. Desperately. Everything she had heard or seen on documentaries and read about India, second hand knowledge at best, could not convince her that it was the same land so many returned Anglo-Indians spoke of, with misty eyes, a faraway look that beheld reverence and romance. She remembered Dennis Hawthorne's lyrical description of India during their stay at Rutherford Hall and then, the severely contrasting documentary film she and Jeremy had gone to see in London. It had portrayed the rampant poverty of the masses and the terrible degrading conditions that prevailed through much of the land; starvation, lack of sanitation and went on to show that millions did not even have basics like a roof over their head or potable water to drink.

The documentary had left Rachel feeling miserable and angry and she had shared her anger with Jeremy, that despite being part of a wealthy empire, for 200 years, the

Indian masses lived in such heart wrenching conditions. Jeremy had corrected her there – 'Not despite, dear, but *because* of the Empire. We've taxed them to the point of starvation for over 200 years and filled our coffers. We've even sold them their own salt, for crying out loud, just so we could profit. Why do you think Gandhi will go down in history as a great man? If it weren't for him, our Empire building types would still be under the misguided notion that we did India a huge favour by ruling over her.'

Well, India had her Independence now. But as Jeremy had pointed out to her, it was a classic case of giving back - too little, too late. India's freedom had come at an enormous cost and her people would pay for it in blood. Recent reports in the news had been of escalating and bestial communal violence due to the impending partition and the formation of Pakistan. Of late, she had been following all news snippets related to India and had recently read in the Times that even the erstwhile optimistic Lord Mountbatten, now feared that the communal monstrosities would be unstoppable and go beyond Gandhi's ken and control despite the immense sway he held over the Indian people.

The Times predicted an out-and-out civil war, on an unprecedented scale within a year. She couldn't believe that in a fortnight's time she would be there, amidst what could possibly turn out to be one of the greatest upheavals in human history. When she mentioned this to Jeremy, in the cabin, he said to her, in between seasick groans, 'We really ought to work on our timing, for future cases, darling.'

Chapter Two

The next day at sea, dawned calm. The sky was still slate grey, but the sea was cold and quiet. By late morning both Jeremy and the Colonel decided to brave the sun deck, and joined Rachel as she ordered her breakfast. Both looked tired and pale after a rough and sleepless night on board.

'Are you sure you don't want anything, darling?' Rachel asked Jeremy, as the smartly uniformed steward took her breakfast order of strong black coffee, two eggs – sunny side up, bacon, toast and marmalade.

Jeremy shook his head and groaned as he lay on the deckchair, covered in a blanket, next to her.

'And what about you, Colonel?'

'Ugh. No, thank you. After last night, I daresay, I've gone off food completely. It's positively indecent of you to offer, my dear. Or to be so cheerful, for that matter, when people around you are close to death,' Colonel Riverton grumbled.

Rachel gave him an indulgent smile and said, 'Oh, come now, Colonel, perhaps a hot cup of tea will get you going again?'

'Alright, make it weak, Steward. No milk, just one sugar.'

As the steward left and the three of them settled back in their reclining deck chairs, Rachel prompted the Colonel into conversation.

'So, Colonel, tell me more about the case,' Rachel said.

'Before I can tell you about the facts surrounding the case, I think it will do you both good to have some background information, about the way things happened and the events leading up to Kitty's murder and the jewel robbery, since the two are interlinked.'

'Sounds fair to me, do go on,' Rachel prompted. She glanced at Jeremy as there was no response from his end. She noticed that he had dozed off.

Colonel Riverton spoke. 'It all really started two years ago, after VE day, when I invited my daughters, Kitty and Angela, along with my son Teddy, to visit me in India for a period of post-war rest and relaxation. I'm not proud of it but I had requested my girls, earlier, once Britain had joined the war, to come and spend the war years in the relative safety and comfort of India but they wouldn't hear of it. You see, my son Teddy had joined the Royal Air Force and the girls too wanted to be actively involved in the war effort back home. Angela eventually worked as a supervisor in a parachute manufacturing factory and Kitty - the more adventurous of the two had actually learnt how to fly a plane! When she wrote and informed me about her new skill as a pilot, you could have knocked me down with a feather.'

'Why, that's fantastic and rather commendable, not to mention very spirited of her.'

'Yes she was rather spirited. Too damned spirited for her own good, as it turned out. The thing is, Rachel, I had sent my girls back home to live with my elder sister Dorothea in Kent, once they were old enough, so they would lead a sheltered life. Flying planes had never once come into the scheme of things I had planned for her future!'

'Yes, I can imagine. When did you send your children to England?'

'About nineteen years ago. Teddy, my eldest was about eight years old when he was accepted at Eton, upon His Highness's recommendation, along with His Highness's first born son, the Crown Prince - Ravindra Richard Dharan or Dickie, as the Prince is affectionately called. The boys – Teddy and Dickie were of the same age and had practically grown up together on the Palace grounds. His Highness felt that it would do them good to study together as well and very generously offered to take care of Teddy's schooling. I daresay royalty or not, it was an intelligent move on his part to make Prince Ravindra's life easier in a strictly English setting. To begin with, the little Indian prince was sure to be completely accepted by the other white boys if he showed up with a white boy as a best friend. Whatever the reasons, it was a golden opportunity for my boy to get an expensive first class education, I could not have dreamt of giving him otherwise. I sent the girls back to England on the same boat as a part of the Royal entourage, to stay with my sister, Dorothea. Kitty was six years old then and Angela had just turned five.'

'Oh, dear, they must have felt quite bereft; having to leave the only home they knew for strange shores, so early in life. '

'Well, initially perhaps, but you know, it is customary for the British in India to send their children back home once they turn five or six. I too, was born in India and sent to stay with relations when I was a child and came back to India to join my regiment, after I had completed my education in England.'

'That is interesting.'

'Yes, the Riverton family has been in India for three generations. Someday, I'll tell you all about it and how I was spotted by the Maharajah and offered this position. It makes for quite an interesting story in itself,' Colonel Riverton paused, as the steward appeared with the breakfast tray and served them.

He continued once the steward had left.

'Anyhow, as I mentioned, the girls could not have stayed on with me. I knew India was no place to bring up two motherless girls and I also had the peace of mind knowing that they would not only be carefully brought up, but also lead a peaceful sheltered life under Dorothea's watchful eyes. For over a decade, that was the case. My sister saw to it that they were brought up with the strictest of conventions and that they attended a good school nearby, for young ladies. I never dreamt that one day they would work outside the home. However, after finishing school, with the onset of the war, all the rules had changed. Like so many young women, my daughters too, went to work and there was nothing Dorothea or anyone, for that matter, could do about it.'

'So Kitty broke the shackles of her strict upbringing and went on to become a pilot,' Rachel said, with undisguised admiration in her voice.

'Yes. As you must know, the shortage of male pilots and mechanics through the war years meant that many young women learned to fly and maintain planes during the war. Kitty was one of them. She trained with Women's Auxiliary Air Force or WAAF and was part of a team that delivered new planes from factories to the military airfields and contributed towards servicing and preparing planes between missions.'

'She sounds like quite a girl to me. I should have liked to know her,' Rachel said, as she plastered marmalade pleasurably over her toast. It was nice to be able to do so without having to worry about the rigours of rationing back home.

'I am certain had you both met, the feeling would have been mutual. I see the same kind of devil-may-care attitude in you, my dear. Fact is, you remind me quite a lot of Kitty. I never thought I'd live to see the day when a young lady as yourself goes about the place in pursuit of criminals and murderers, albeit successfully, as I've been given to believe. Pardon me, but it seems to me a highly dangerous thing for any woman to do. I may sound rather old school to you but honestly, what is the world coming to?'

'To a far better place, Colonel, as far as women are concerned. Or would you rather we all sat quietly in a room somewhere and did needlework?' Rachel responded with a mischievous smile.

Colonel Riverton sighed, 'Ah, well, no. I should have thought that women had quite enough to do at home and hearth but then, they say we would've never won the war without the contribution from our women. Seems to me, the world is changing right before my eyes and I suppose the old school of thought must change to accommodate the new order.'

'Quite so, Colonel. Where were we? Yes, you were saying that Teddy, Kitty and Angela came out to India in 1945...'

'Yes, they set sail August end and were in India by mid September. I could not go personally to receive them, since I was in the thick of training and preparing the Royal teams and horses for the onset of the polo season, which begins in October. The Palace staff, mostly the old retainers were quite excited about their arrival, and so was the Prince. He told me that he was looking forward to being reunited with his childhood friends. When I informed him that I was too busy to go to Bombay, he sent one of his most trusted Khidmatgars, er, that means a royal bearer, by the way, to receive them in Bombay and accompany them to Dharanpore. They arrived after a dusty two day train journey, just in time to attend a State dinner at the Dharanpore Palace given in the joint honour of Prince Dickie's twenty fifth birthday and the birth of his first son, which is a grand occasion in any royal family.'

At that moment, Jeremy woke up and asked in a groggy voice, 'Did I miss much?'

Rachel smiled and said, 'You may want to stay awake for this, Jeremy. I suspect this case is going to be quite an interesting one.'

Chapter Three

Jeremy listened as Rachel briefly recounted what the Colonel had told her and then addressed the Colonel, 'Getting back to the Prince's twenty-fifth birthday party, I've heard that Indian royalty entertain on a grand scale. Is that true?'

'Oh yes! On a truly grand scale, the likes of which, we don't see very often, even in the Royal Houses of Europe, come to think of it. For the Prince's birthday, for example, preparations had been made on a mammoth scale. Guests came from all over the Empire, including high ranking British officers and their wives, well placed Indians, ICS Officers, the Maharajahs of other Princely States and His Highness' personal friends from Europe, who were invited to a week-long lavish stay at the Palace. Nearly two hundred of these guests were accommodated within the Palace itself, for a week of tiger shooting, riding, fishing and a host of other royal events including a polo match.

The event was flagged off by an eight course sit-down dinner in the Palace for two hundred and fifty guests. On the same evening, over seven thousand Dharanpore subjects were given a veritable feast on the Palace grounds. It was a week-long royal banquet to end all others, what with jewelled elephants lined up at the palace steps to greet guests, and splendidly uniformed armed guards with scarlet turbans, lining the palace hallways and staircases.

That first night, I remember, before dinner, the royal musicians set up in the Marble Palace and played Indian music as the dancing girls set the tone with their ghungroos, er, tinkling musical anklets. Amidst all this noise and pomp, the Prince arrived in his full formal state regalia, dripping with jewels from his silk turbaned head right down to the embellished shoes on his feet. He looked wonderful and seemed to me the very embodiment of Indian royalty. And although it was September, the air was balmy. It was such a magical evening. But, *that* was the night the trouble started.'

'Trouble?'

'Oh, yes. When I look back I realise it was the same night, which set in motion the events that eventually led to Kitty's murder,' he paused to take a sip of tea, as Jeremy and Rachel looked at him expectantly, awaiting the rest of the narration.

He continued, 'It was evident from the evening of the Royal banquet that Kitty was quite literally the 'belle of the ball'. Nothing had prepared any of us for her appearance. When I had last seen her, she had been a chubby little girl with freckles and two missing front teeth! I don't know what I had expected, but I had rather envisioned from her letters to me that she would be a tomboy strutting about dressed in manly clothes. So you can imagine my pride and joy, when I saw that my daughter had in fact turned into what most men would consider, a raging beauty. The adventure of flying planes through the war had obviously done her good and given her a certain air of confidence. Other than that, she seemed to have a rather conservative and delicate taste in dressing that met my approval.'

Rachel piped up, 'Ooh, that does sound interesting. Not that it has any bearing on the case but do you remember what she wore for the banquet?'

'Women! I'll never understand their fascination with clothes! Well, I can't tell you exactly but I do remember that she wore one of those golden gossamer gown things that women like to wear at these do's and looked positively ethereal. I daresay that I was a tad bit concerned that so many men flocked around her like bees around a honey-pot but she seemed quite blasé to the kind of admiration she was drawing and was handling herself rather well. I secretly nurtured a hope that she would find a husband amongst the august gathering of some of India's finest ICS bachelors and single British officers present at the banquet. I hadn't much hope for Angela, who I daresay had turned out to be quite a Plain Jane with spectacles and looked more like a dressed up librarian than anything else. She seemed quite uneasy and uncomfortable in such a glittering setting, whilst her sister made the most of it.'

Rachel spoke, 'But I seem to recall you told us, at The Savoy that your daughter Angela got married at a decent interval soon after Kitty's death and now lives in Kensington with her husband and the twins. So your fears were obviously unfounded.'

'Yes, that's the dashed thing about human nature. It was Angela who managed to bag one of Kitty's many admirers – a most sought after ICS bachelor, a chap by the name of Arthur Blackwell. In fact Arthur, as I recall, had proposed to Kitty and they were even engaged for a very brief period, till he realised that he was getting nowhere with Kitty and that her affections lay elsewhere. He then broke off their engagement and transferred his attentions to Angela. I don't mean to be uncharitable but God knows what he saw in Angela! Anyhow they got married soon after that.'

Rachel spoke, 'So ironically, 'Plain Jane' Angela did in fact turn out to be the smart one, while beautiful Kitty ended up getting romantically entangled with the Prince and wound up in a most unfortunate, doomed relationship.'

Jeremy cut in, 'But what about the royal wife in this equation - Princess Uma Devi? Wasn't she at this banquet too?'

'That's just it. The Princess had given birth, ten days prior to that and was confined in a traditional twenty eight day ceremonial seclusion along with her new born son. As per Rajput custom, she was ensconced within the walls of the zenana. And although she had given up Purdah, she did follow the traditional rituals that followed childbirth to a 'T'.

'Oh dear, the Prince sounds like quite a cad,' Rachel blurted out.

The Colonel smiled and said, 'Between you and me dear, I do believe that most men of royal lineage usually are, where women are concerned, until proven innocent. And I have yet to come across a royal who doesn't maintain a sizeable harem in India.'

'Really, even in this day and age?'

'Oh, yes! Rumour has it that even the physically unprepossessing Nizam of Hyderabad currently maintains a harem of over two hundred women.'

'No!'

'Yes! And one hears that the erstwhile ruler of Patiala State, the robust Maharajah Bhupinder Singh had double the number of wives and concubines. And his sons followed suit.'

Jeremy spoke up, 'Goodness! And I have enough trouble maintaining one wife! Where do these chaps get their stamina from, I wonder.' He chuckled as Rachel rolled her eyes at him.

'I think it is more about maintaining the royal image and prestige than actual...er... visits to the harem,' the Colonel said, trying to put it as delicately as he could for Rachel's benefit.

'Oh never mind the harem, Colonel. Getting back to that evening. Tell us what happened after that?' Rachel asked.

'I sensed there was trouble brewing when the Prince couldn't keep his eyes off Kitty. Although, I was somewhat relieved that Kitty, on her part, seemed not to notice. But, I suppose women are incalculable,' he said with a sigh.

'What makes you say that, Colonel?' Jeremy asked with a smile.

'You see, I managed to get a hold of her diary after her death, in which she clearly states that although they hardly managed to exchange more than a few formal lines in conversation, the stolen glances between 'Dickie' and herself dominated her entire evening and she spent the rest of it in a dizzy girlish haze of love at first sight! Incalculable, I tell you!'

'So, there is a diary!' Rachel exclaimed and continued, 'May I read it? It may help me to better understand the events leading up to Kitty's death. Of course, that is, only if you feel, it's is not too personal a request.'

'Not at all, my dear. If you really wish to read it, I shall hand it over to you tonight. Although I must warn you that it is choc-a-bloc full of silly girlish nonsense and not much else. She describes the tiger shoot, boating trips and the royal picnics they went on and so on. Romantic descriptions of events through the rose tinted glasses of a foolish young girl in love and that sort of thing.'

'Oh, thank you, Colonel. I may find something that needs a woman's interpretation, something a no-nonsense man like you may have missed,' Rachel said, reminiscing over the past two cases she had successfully solved at Rutherford Hall and Ravenrock House, based on the strength of the much berated and sometimes illogical 'woman's intuition.'

'Oh, I flipped through it and read about a quarter of it before I realised that I couldn't stomach anymore of that guff. So, if there is anything in the diary, which I doubt, I'm sure you'll find it. Right. Where were we?'

'At the Prince's week long birthday banquet.'

'Ah, yes. Anyhow, as the days went by and people started talking, I tackled Kitty one evening and didn't bother to mince my words. I told her she was behaving like a fool and that if she continued in the same way she would, in all likelihood end up like the notorious Anita Delgado, or worse, Florry Bryan.'

'Can't say I've heard of them,' Jeremy said.

'Isn't Anita Delgado the famous Spanish princess?' Rachel asked.

'Hardly a princess, hmph! She was an uneducated Spanish flamenco dancer from an impoverished background, who caught the eye of the Maharajah of Kapurthala, while he was on holiday in Spain. He took a fancy to her, married her and brought her back to India with him as his fifth Maharani, much against the will of the Kapurthala Royal family and the powers that be of British India. You see, neither the high caste royal Hindus and Sikhs, nor the British approve of such inter-racial alliances. In consequence, for a while, she led a wretched albeit wealthy life, intensely despised by the very family she had married into. To make matters worse, the Maharajah eventually lost interest in her and she fled from him and the constant hostility she faced in the Palace.

Of course, inside information from the Kapurthala camp paints quite a different picture. Some say she got bored to death and started having affairs and that the Maharajah threw her out because of her blatant adultery.

She is said to have had numerous affairs, right under his nose, including the notorious one with her own stepson - the Maharajah's son from an older Maharani. From all accounts, she led a scandalous life in India and now lives somewhere in Europe as an exile, divorced, poor and stripped of her royal title. Forced to move from place to place and man to man like a rudderless boat.'

'That's some story. And what about Florry Bryan. Who was she?' Rachel asked.

'A common English girl whose brother Charles Bryan took care of the Stables of His Highness, Rajinder Singh – the Maharajah of Patiala. It is rumoured that the philandering Maharajah seduced her whilst she was visiting her brother in India. The Maharajah did eventually marry her but only after she was five months pregnant, carrying his child. Made her change her religion and renamed her Harnam Kaur. She too, was despised and alienated by both the Sikh nobility and the British alike. It is said that her baby was poisoned to death by the Maharajah's other wives in a Palace intrigue and that she herself died or was poisoned sometime soon after that.'

'Ugh. Poisoned babies, murderous in-laws. You seem to have a repertoire of sad, not to mention gruesome stories, Colonel.'

'Well, these are not stories but actual recorded facts and the one thing they all have in common is that, it never ends well when a white woman marries an Indian, even if he is a royal. It never has and probably never will. I was just trying to get that into my daughter's fat head.'

'Let me guess, these stories... er... my apologies, these 'actual recorded facts' didn't make much of an impression on her, or did they?' Rachel asked, tongue-in-cheek.

'No, they bally well didn't! On the contrary she gave me some humbug that times had changed and this was different and that I knew nothing about true love. And that she would be fine as long as she could be with her prince till her dying day. At any rate, she got her wish. She was dead within a fortnight.'

Chapter Four

They met in the evening at the ship's lounge bar. RMS Arundel had crossed the Straits of Gibraltar and was now moving through the calm waters of the Mediterranean Sea. Apart from a gentle rolling motion that Rachel found quite soothing, the ship was sailing smoothly.

It was dark outside and the lounge was lit by shaded lamps, which threw a soft golden light across the wood panelled room and apart from a few other passengers, they had the entire bar to themselves. The Colonel was true to his words and handed over a leather bound journal to Rachel.

'There you go. That's Kitty's diary. Hope you can find something in there that will throw some light on this case. I wouldn't count on it though. I certainly couldn't decipher anything from the romantic mush that's on every bally page! Whatever little I read, I must admit that she gave a colourful picture of what the banquet and royal events were like. You'll probably enjoy the descriptions even if you find nothing else of value in it,' he said, as he sank into a leather armchair and signalled the steward.

'Why, thank you, Colonel,' Rachel said, with gratitude in her voice. 'I'm sure, I will. I hope to find something more in this. I'll set aside some time to start reading it tomorrow.'

As the steward brought their cocktails, Rachel addressed the Colonel, 'I've been meaning to ask you something.'

'Yes?'

'From your narration so far, I gather that the Prince was already married and had a child by his twenty-fifth birthday?'

'Not one my dear, but two children. Oh yes. He was betrothed to Uma Devi - a Rajput Princess in a royal alliance ever since he was thirteen and his bride-to-be was five. Their first child was a daughter.'

'Why! That's child marriage!' Rachel said aloud.

'Not quite, I've put it across in my own muddled way, I suppose. You see, just as in England, the royal families in India have marriage alliances with other royal families, to strengthen their combined wealth, prestige and political power. The Prince and Princess were betrothed as children but were wed according to Hindu custom only after she had concluded her education in England. By the end of it, the little princess Uma Devi was fluent in English, French and German, widely travelled and quite well read. She was seventeen at the time of the royal wedding. And quite accomplished and mature as per Indian or even Victorian standards, if you ask me.'

'I'll say! That is interesting. And the Maharajah was not concerned that his daughter-in-law received a modern western education?' Jeremy asked.

'No. You see, it was His Highness, the Maharajah Paramjit Dharan who had insisted upon it. He is far ahead of his times and is all for progress in Dharanpore. He has travelled the world and wants to better the conditions of his people and the State by building better hospitals, schools and roads, thereby giving his people access to better health and education.'

'He sounds like an enlightened ruler.'

'He is. Or should I say, was. He abdicated the throne to his son last year, owing to the fact that he suffers from ill health and now lives in Switzerland. He is undergoing treatment there and is too weak to travel back and forth to India. The Crown Prince – Prince Dickie has completely taken over the day to day running of the State, although in deference to his father, he has not taken the title of 'Maharajah' yet and will not do so until the old man passes away.'

'That's rather considerate of him,' Rachel said.

'You know, there is a misconception in the West about Eastern Rulers. Most people assume that they are despotic and unenlightened. But that's far from the truth. Eastern subjects have a tremendous reverence for their 'annadata' or king and provider, well, apart from the fact that they believe they are divinely ordained to rule, but mostly because they tend to also be just and wise. And the majority of rulers do love their subjects and work towards their welfare. Take the Maharajah of Mysore, for example. I mean, you just have to visit the State of Mysore to see the amazing change he has brought about for the betterment of his people.

Now getting back to our Maharajah Paramjit Dharan – I've heard him say, time and again that progress can never come completely to any state, if half the population consisting of women are left uneducated and backward. To begin with, a few years ago, he wanted to remove the Purdah system, which was widely prevalent among Royal ladies and the high caste households in Dharanpore at the time. But that's easier said than done. To that end, he had insisted that his future daughter-in-law, the Princess Uma should receive a western upbringing and education, so that she could lead by example – be a paragon of sorts, for furthering education and emancipation of women in the State. And simultaneously be the perfect consort for his Eton educated son – Dickie. It was important to him that she be perfectly at ease when it came to mingling with Europeans.'

'Why? Did they have a lot of dealings with Europeans?' Rachel queried.

'My dear, they did and they still do. Before Independence, they had constant dealings with the Empire apart from Durbars and State occasions. Except through the war years, the royal family spent six months in Europe, every year. Most of the high level staff including myself, consist of Europeans. And back then, the Maharajah felt and rightly so, that an educated princess could be a great support to his son – the Crown Prince in running the State, if India were to ever regain her Independence from the Empire.'

Jeremy spoke, 'But I was given to believe that Dharanpore was never directly a part of the Empire.'

'You are right to some extent. I daresay, it may sound confusing but let me try to explain. The British Crown or its representative Viceroy ruled over two very different Indias. The first was about three-fifths of the subcontinent, which was governed directly as British India. The second, the 'Indian India', so to speak, were the Royal Indian States that together comprised of close to 565 princely states covering approximately over 965,000 square kilometres. Due to the sheer numbers of Royal Indian States, and their diversity in terms of sizes and revenues, the British had to devise a grading system for the Rulers in the form of 'gun salutes'. I mean, how else do you differentiate between a ruler, such as the Nizam of Hyderabad, who has dominion over 130,000 square kilometres, a population of over fourteen million, with an annual revenue recorded at eighty-five million rupees, and Chief or Thakur of a statelet of let's say, the Kathiawar with less than sixteen square kilometres, about five hundred subjects and an annual revenue of ten thousand rupees or less?'

'Hmm. I see your point. And you say there were over 560 of them? I'm betting, the chap who had to allocate gun salutes went raving mad after doing the job,' Rachel grinned.

'My dear, the task was not upto one man, but the entire Indian Civil Service. To begin with, there were the First division States, 118 of them, to be precise. These were known as the Salute States. Their rank being measured by gun salutes fired on all formal occasions, descending in odd numbers from 21, down to 9. Below those came the Non-Salute States, 117 of them, which enjoyed a limited jurisdiction and full relations with the Government of India, followed by over three hundred hereditary landowners, namely Zamindars, Talukdars, Thanedars, Thakurs and Jagirdars, the eastern equivalent of European Counts, Barons, Earls, Lords and so on. Their estates were under the civil and criminal jurisdiction of the 'Political Agent', appointed by the Viceroy. Some non salute rulers, as the Maharajahs of Burdwan and Darbhanga were fabulously wealthy. However, officially they were not considered as pukka Princes, even by other Indian Maharajas and had no role to play in the Chamber of Princes. My dear, I apologise - this must be quite boring for you?' He said, addressing Rachel.

She replied, 'Oh, no, Colonel, I ought to be the one to apologise if my eyes glazed over. Apart from the number of cocktails I seem to have imbibed, I was never one for numbers or history lessons. Mostly, they have the incredible effect of putting me to sleep in record time, but this is interesting as I'm assuming that this does somehow relate to the case. So where does Dharanpore stand, in the scheme of things such as gun salutes and the rest of it?'

'Ah, I was just coming to that. That was just a prelude to give you some background information and an idea of the importance and official standing, the State of Dharanpore enjoys. It is a First Division, 17-Gun State, comprising of twenty two thousand square kilometres and the ruler is a bonafide member of the Chamber of Princes', Colonel Riverton said, unable to mask the pride in his voice.

Jeremy needed clarification. 'So, let me get this straight. What you mean is that even during the Raj, the Royal State of Dharanpore was independent of the British Empire?'

'Well yes and no. Technically the State of Dharanpore, like its other Royal counterparts, was considered foreign territory, as far as the British Empire was concerned. However, these royal Indian States, though independent in governance, were expected to be in perpetual alliance and friendship with Britain and owed ultimate allegiance to the King-Emperor or Queen-Empress.'

Jeremy asked, 'And what does that translate to? Are you trying to say that these rulers were, in reality, puppet rulers under British governance?'

'Not quite. Each ruler had complete authority and freedom to run his State as he pleased with only a minimal touch of interference from the British, in the form of a British Political Agent. The idea was that this British officer would keep an eye on the going-ons in the State without ever actually directly interfering with governance. In most cases, the Political Officer appointed by the Viceroy was a friendly aide to the ruler, unless of course, the occasion called for interference, such as cases of gross misrule, mismanagement or injustice on part of the ruler but this was extremely rare. The only example that comes to my mind was the deposition of the Maharajah of Alwar, in the thirties, more than a decade ago. His cruelty towards his subjects had given him an unsurpassed notoriety that had invoked the powers of paramountcy - the Viceroy through his political agents, who eventually deposed the ruler. But I digress. Once you get me started about India, I can go on for hours and hours.'

Rachel spoke, 'I must congratulate you on your encyclopaedic knowledge of the Indian princely states, Colonel. It's really quite amazing.'

'Thank you, my dear. As I mentioned, my family has been here for three generations. It's only natural that one picks up interesting bits and pieces of information along the way,' he said with a smile.

'I'd like to know how you came to settle in Dharanpore,' Rachel asked.

'It's a long story my dear and I will certainly share it with you another day. But for now, I must take your leave. We will continue, where we left off, tomorrow,' Colonel Riverton said, as he heaved himself out of the leather armchair.

'Why, what are you upto, Colonel? Off on a romantic rendezvous, a secret shipboard romance, perhaps?' Rachel asked with a grin.

'No such luck, my dear. As it turns out, I have a mundane appointment with the Ship's galley. I have to see to Princess Uma Devi's menu preparations for tomorrow. She is a strict vegetarian and as such, always has a high caste Indian cook who accompanies her. I must make sure that when they come aboard in Marseilles, there will be adequate provisions set aside for her and the other members of the entourage who are also vegetarian.'

'I wonder how they survived six months in post war Europe on a strictly vegetarian diet. The rationing is rigorous enough for a normal diet,' Rachel mused.

The Colonel answered, 'Oh, they stay at places like The Savoy in London and The Majestic at Monte Carlo. I assure you, their every need is taken care of. But the Princess is rather strict about her meals being prepared by an upper caste Brahmin cook. You see, according to the Hindu caste system, we Europeans fall under the category of 'untouchables'.'

'Ooh. I don't fancy being classified as an untouchable. Why on earth, would Europeans be considered as untouchables in India?'

'For the simple reason that we eat both beef and pork, the former being considered holy and the latter unholy. What can I say, it's a complicated culture. But the Indians are extremely hospitable people. So is the Princess. She is just terribly particular about her personal diet.'

Rachel piped up, 'It's funny that western education hasn't managed to change her mind-set around that.'

'My dear, a decade of learning in the West can hardly be expected to erase a three thousand year old cultural doctrine.'

Jeremy spoke, 'I quite agree and nor should it. Cultural heritage is a valuable possession and I respect the Princess for sticking to her guns. This goes to prove that one can learn much from another man's culture without having to let go of one's own set of values.'

Rachel smiled and said, 'This is why I love you, Jeremy. Your perspective is, as always, interesting. And I suppose the world would be a rather dull place if we all did, spoke and ate the same things, all of the time.'

Chapter Five

At Marseilles, the Dharanpore Royals came on board along with their entourage. Rachel had joined Colonel Riverton and the ship's Captain, as they waited to greet the royal family. As Princess Uma Devi made her way up the gangplank followed by a retinue of mostly European female staff, Rachel was quite taken aback by the Princess' alabaster skin and fragile beauty. She had expected to see a robust dusky Indian lady with kohl lined eyes. Instead, the Princess looked like a pale European aristocrat with a head of shingled dark hair. There was an undoubted regal grace about her. Even from a distance, one could make out that she was a blue-blooded royal. There was a chill in the air and the princess came aboard wrapped in a luxurious fur coat, which covered her full length draped chiffon dress that Rachel assumed to be the Indian sari.

Colonel Riverton greeted the Princess as soon as she came onto deck and introduced her to Rachel. 'Welcome aboard, Your Highness. This is Lady Rachel Markham, niece of the late Sir Charles Rutherford, who I am given to believe, you were acquainted with,' Colonel Riverton said smoothly.

'Good afternoon, Colonel,' the Princess said, in a flawless British accent and then turning towards Rachel, she said, 'And I am delighted to meet you, Lady Markham. Your uncle was a dear friend of mine. Do accept my condolences on his passing. He shall be sorely missed. And I have heard about you, from the good Colonel here. By all accounts, you seem to be a gifted and courageous young lady. Do give me some time to settle in and then I shall welcome you to my stateroom where we can have a little chat.'

'It would be my pleasure, Your Highness,' Rachel said, with a small curtsey.

'My dear, let's not stand on formalities. We have a long voyage ahead together. Please feel free to call me Uma.'

'Then, I look forward to our meeting, Princess Uma.'

As she walked by, Rachel turned to the Colonel with a raised eyebrow and whispered, 'Really, *Lady Rachel Markham?*'

'My dear, if you want the Princess to take you seriously, she must be made aware of your aristocratic lineage.'

'She didn't seem like a snob to me, on the contrary...'

'Tsk, tsk, you have a lot to learn about Indian Royals yet, my dear.'

Then he turned as he saw the Prince make his way up the gangplank. He was smartly dressed in what seemed to be, a perfectly cut Savile Row suit. He was followed by four young Indian men dressed alike in European clothes. Rachel gasped and thought to herself, if there was a walking embodiment of the clichéd 'tall, dark and handsome', it was the Prince. As he reached them and the Colonel made introductions, the Prince took her hand in a smooth gesture, kissed it as he held her eyes in his powerfully hypnotic gaze and said in a deep, polished voice, 'Charmed, I'm sure,' before he moved on to meet the ship's Captain. Rachel was charmed alright and she could instinctively see why Kitty had not listened to reason.

Now that she had seen the leading characters in the drama, Rachel couldn't wait to start reading Kitty's journal. She put on a warm coat and took it with her to the upper deck, where she knew she would not be disturbed for an hour or two. Once she went up the steps, she realised that although the sea was calm, it was a very windy day. She pulled up her coat collar and curled up on a deck chair in the far corner and began reading.

As with any reading material, by force of habit, Rachel briefly flipped through the journal in its entirety before she began reading in earnest. To her relief, she noticed that this particular journal was only half full and had quite obviously been dedicated to Kitty's travel back to India after nearly two decades. Kitty's flowing handwriting was for the most part legible although in some places where she had scribbled in a hurry, it would take a while for anyone to decipher the meaning and interpret the doodles that were scattered liberally throughout the pages.

She almost giggled aloud at Kitty's artistic attempt at sketching what seemed to be a large cat lying in the grass and then read the inscription below - *A ferocious Indian tiger Teddy shot the day before.* To Rachel's mind, the tiger in the sketch looked more like a large grumpy feline not unlike King George - Mrs. Hopworth's cat at Rutherford Hall. Mrs. Hopworth was the cook at the Hall and she had insisted on naming the ginger tom, 'King George' in deference to what she claimed to be - his regal bearing. King George, on his part had other ideas and went on to stupefy them all. Much to Mrs. Hopworth's consternation and to everyone else's amusement, with what seemed like a careless disregard for his royal status and name, King George had proceeded to give birth to litter after litter until it was finally spayed by the local vet.

Smiling to herself, Rachel started reading the journal from the first page. It was filled with, as the Colonel had described, the excited ramblings of a girl who started out with unabridged delight to revisit her childhood in an exotic land that had all but faded away, in her memory. It described the voyage by sea and then the shock of seeing the teeming masses of humanity at Bombay port.

She wrote about all that she saw - the coolies, the beggars, the shrieking vendors, the dust, the heat and most of all, the sheer noisiness of it all.

It is the din of thousands of raised voices, people shouting in incomprehensible dialects in all directions that carries far on the hot breeze. I had forgotten what a loud country India is! As we waited our turn to go down the gangplank, I could see uniformed white men in hats, escorting memsahibs carrying parasols, making their way through the vast crowds of Indian coolies and sweetmeat, fruit and vegetable vendors dressed in white and cream dhotis. Under the glaring sun, the bright colours of the saris worn by dark skinned women - in shrill pink, parrot green, iridescent blue, gleaming purple and flame orange, dazzle my eyes. And the cornucopia of smells! I can't even begin to describe the heady mix of spices, open sewers, roasting gram, smoke, stale sweat and urine that assails and overpowers one as soon as you prepare to get off the boat!

There were a few pages on their hot and dusty train journey where Kitty had described how despite changing clothes thrice a day, she still wound up feeling grimy. And although there were three layers of plate glass and slatted Venetian blinds to keep out the Sun's glare, it didn't do them much good. According to Kitty, everything seemed to be covered in a fine layer of black coal dust as the coal fired steam engine made its way through the hot and dusty landscape of India's countryside. Their trusty Khidmatgar – Bahadur Singh did his best by changing their sheets and pillowcases with fresh ones every evening but they still wound waking up in dark grey sheets by morning.

Kitty also wrote about her co-passengers.

This is a fine traveling party! Teddy has been grumpy throughout. He keeps saying he doesn't fancy Indian weather, as if the rest of us are cooing over the climate here. And oh, dear Mother of God, I'd do anything if you could spare me Angela's morose outlook on life. It's been over a year since her fellow – Jim, died across enemy lines and she still hasn't gotten over him. Well, I suppose it's hard for someone like Angela to find a fellow in the first place so my telling her there's plenty of other fish in the sea is obviously not going to help!

But her moping isn't helping anyone either including poor old dead Jim who was such a cheerful chap. It was his own fault that he enlisted as an SOE. He had no business attempting to be a spy, in the first place. He couldn't stop blabbering to Angela and me about his dangerous undercover mission in France! And I thought that spies were supposed to be the strong and silent types. He was possibly the most indiscreet spy I've ever come across. As far as I am concerned he signed his own death warrant.

Anyhow never mind the war, it's all over now. I am so excited to be back in India and can't wait to see what the Dharanpore Palace looks like now. I'm staring out the window as we chug along and I think I've just spotted the skinniest cow I've ever laid eyes on! She looks like she could do with some grass but I haven't seen a meadow for miles. As far as the eye can see, the landscape is positively desolate, well apart from a scattering of thorn trees. Wonder what these poor animals survive on.

Making a mental note to ask Colonel Riverton more about Angela's Jim, Rachel skipped a few pages that described in detail, the villages and livestock they passed and the stops they made on the railway line, till she came to the part where Kitty wrote about their arrival at Dharanpore Palace and the royal banquet.

I feel quite human again after a long soak in the gorgeous sunken marble tub. For a while back there, I thought I would never be able to wash off all the dirt and grime that I seem to have collected on the rail journey but time and patience and most importantly, a luxurious quantity of sweet smelling bath salts and fancy French soap has restored my faith infinitely. Judging from the guest bath amenities alone, one can safely assume that the Maharajah obviously does entertain on a truly lavish scale! The Palace is truly wonderful. And oh, the baths here are to die for! I never expected modern plumbing or electric light in this ancient edifice but oh, I am so grateful for it. The bath fixtures and taps are all golden, the enamel throne is comfortable and there's even a matching bidet!

The Amah must have been quite amused to see me coo over them, so she explained in a combination of her own brand of broken English and sign language that these modern attached baths are a new addition to this wing and that the Maharajah had everything specially imported and fixed just in time for this event, in honour of his European guests. Anyhow, she's seen to my unpacking and I've asked her to lay out my best dress, the champagne chiffon. I think I shall wear my creamy pearls with it. I'm so glad I sprung for a new wardrobe last minute, even though it cost the earth! But this has to be my favourite dress amongst them all. It really is quite gorgeous and I am quite sure that floating about in it, I'm going to feel rather like a pampered princess myself and be right at home at the royal banquet! For now, a nap is in order. There's still plenty of time before the festivities begin. And a girl needs her beauty sleep!

The next entry in the diary described the banquet hall in detail. The glittering marble halls embellished with the Royal Dharanpore coat of arms, the liveried bearers, the aristocratic guests, the hors d'oeuvres, the champagne and cocktails served before dinner and finally the Prince's dramatic entrance.

'When they announced Dickie's arrival with a great deal of pomp and trumpeting, every eye in the room was on the entrance and in walked this gorgeous Indian Prince. You could have knocked me down with a feather. I could not believe that the little brown boy with scraped elbows and knees, who used to join forces with Teddy to torment my sister and me, had turned into this wonderfully handsome bejewelled Prince who stood before us. Such a majestic man! Such self assurance and dignity! For want of a better description, Dickie in his new avatar is quite possibly the most beautiful man I have ever set my eyes on.

He stood at the entrance flanked by his smart ADCs and his eyes scanned the room and the guests. I was standing towards the right of the entrance so it took a while for him to notice me but when he did, I realised that his eyes were on me. And then the moment when our eyes locked for the first time, I could feel my knees go weak. I saw him whisper to his aide, who glanced at me and whispered something back in his ears. From there on the evening took on a dream like haze. I vaguely remember that there were hundreds of other people in the glittering room and that I did make some perfunctory dinner and post-dinner conversation with some British officers and other guests but really, the entire evening all I could feel was Dickie's blazing gaze that made my heart beat faster and the blood rush through my veins. And I rather fancy that my brain stopped functioning altogether.

I swear that if anyone had told me even an hour before... that 'love at first sight' was something that I would experience in my lifetime, I would have laughed *my head off. I always assumed that sort of thing only happened with girls who were a little soft in the head. But there it is. I am officially in love, that too 'at first sight', madly and passionately so, and if it weren't for Dickie's marital status I'd be happy to scream about it from every single rooftop in Dharanpore! Anyhow, I am ashamed to say that I almost swooned (another first for me!) when he stood right before me at arm's-length, kissed my hand, looked deep in my eyes, smiled and said in a husky meaningful voice, 'It's so good to have you back, Kitty. You look so radiant tonight, all the lights in this room pale in comparison. I think you were born to light up a Palace. Welcome home to Dharanpore.' I think I managed to mumble something inane back at him, I was so tongue tied! And it was in that instant, looking into his eyes that I knew that we were made to be together and that I was 'home'. Don't ask me mundane questions like 'how' or 'why' because I shall have no answer.*

All I know is that if any other man under the Sun had the gumption to inform me that I was born to light up a Palace, I would have sweetly but surely quipped back, 'Like Edison's light bulb, you mean?' And all I know is that when Dickie said it, I didn't have any smart comebacks. It was like he meant it from his heart and I knew it to be true, from mine.

At that point, Rachel stopped reading and looked up to see a Steward coming towards her. He addressed her, 'A message for you, Madam,' and presented her a silver salver on which a monogrammed card had been placed. She thanked the steward as she took the card and read the message, which duly informed her that Her Highness, Princess Uma Devi had requested the pleasure of her company in her stateroom.

Chapter Six

Rachel found the Princess' stateroom door unlocked as she knocked and announced her arrival.

'Do come in, Lady Markham and make yourself at home,' Princess Uma said, with a wave of her jewelled hand. She was seated at her writing desk and had her back to the door. She seemed to be in the middle of some correspondence.

'I could come back later, if you are busy, Princess,' Rachel offered as she glanced around. The sheer size and luxury of the Princess' stateroom made the cabin she shared with Jeremy seem like a matchbox, albeit a comfortable matchbox.

'Not at all. I was just wading through the never ending task of responding to one's seemingly endless acquaintances around the world. People are so kind but you must know how tedious that can get sometimes.

It will be a relief to spend some time with you instead,' she said, as she capped and put her fountain pen down. She then turned to give Rachel her full attention.

Rachel noted that the princess was dressed in a pastel pink chiffon sari with pearls around her throat and large teardrop solitaires on her earlobes. And she was even more fragile and beautiful, almost flawlessly so, at close quarters. She smiled at the princess and said, 'I can quite imagine that royal duties take up a great deal of your time.'

'They do but it is the price one must pay for the role one is entrusted with, so I don't mind it, really. May I offer you some tea, Lady Markham?'

'Thank you, Princess. A cup of hot tea would be perfect. I've just come down from the upper deck, where I was reading for the better part of an hour and I never realised that my bones had gone quite so cold.'

'Ah, yes. There is a decided nip in the air. Thankfully, our staterooms are heated,' the Princess said, as she rang a little silver bell on her desk and a French maid appeared through a connecting door. She was duly dispatched to get some refreshments.

'So Lady Markham, I understand that this is your first trip to India?'

'Yes, indeed Princess. In fact it is my first trip aboard an ocean liner of this size.'

'Really? In that case, I do hope that it has been a comfortable journey so far and that the Colonel has been looking after you and your husband.'

'Absolutely. We couldn't have asked for more. It is very kind of you to ask.'

'Not at all, my dear. It is my duty to ensure your comfort given that you both have kindly agreed to come all the way to India to help us out with our little spot of trouble.'

Rachel smiled as she thought to herself how perceptions differed. Not many people would classify a murder and a major jewel heist within their home, as a 'little spot of trouble.'

'Lady Markham, may I be frank with you?'

'Certainly but I would feel a lot more at ease if you called me Rachel, Princess Uma.'

'Then my dear, Rachel, is what I shall call you. You see, we are both ladies with a certain pedigree and belong to a certain class. And as such, I am sure that you will agree with me when I say that breeding counts. Unfortunately the woman, who got killed in our Palace, had none. I believe she was a working woman...'

'Yes. She flew planes through the war, Princess,' Rachel said out loud, whilst thinking to herself that the Colonel had been spot-on about the Princess being a snob under the camouflage of her obvious charm.

The Princess continued, 'And I am told she also did the work of an airplane mechanic. Some say she was an adventuress and a social climber. Women like that get can get into extraordinary messes themselves and make things quite difficult for people around them.'

'Like getting murdered in other people's homes?'

The Princess laughed, 'I see you do understand. Well that, among other things.'

'Such as?'

'Oh, come now, I am sure you would have heard by now that this woman formed an unhealthy fascination for my husband, the Prince. I suppose she saw it as an opportunity to better her station in life by forcing some sort of an alliance with him.'

'Did she?' Rachel asked, feigning ignorance.

'I am sorry to say that yes, I was told she attempted every possible trick in the book to trap my husband into an illicit affair and men as we both know, can be such fools when it comes to deciphering the wiles of a woman like that.'

'I haven't had that experience yet, Princess. My husband has not given me the opportunity so far.'

'You probably haven't been married long enough, my dear Rachel,' the Princess replied with a smile.

'I can't argue with that, Princess. We are yet to celebrate our first anniversary.'

'That is sweet. I remember our first year of marriage was quite idyllic. My husband whisked me away to some of the most beautiful places in Europe, on a whirlwind honeymoon that lasted over six months,' the Princess said with a faraway look, dreamily reminiscing over the first flush of love and her romantic honeymoon.

Rachel grinned and said, 'Well, I must admit that Jeremy and I didn't do anything quite so grand but I did take my husband to Dartmouth on a honeymoon he's not likely to forget any time soon.' She smiled as she thought to herself, it would be a miracle if he forgot the extraordinary circumstances of their trip to Dartmouth and their quest to catch a ruthless killer there.

'So you do understand my concerns with this case?'

'I am sorry, Princess but I'm afraid you've lost me there.'

'Rachel, I feel I ought to warn you that everything is not as it seems. And that you must not believe everything you hear. Fact is, my husband, like most men, may be flattered for a while by attentions from such a woman and even go as far to have a little passing romance but like myself, he is a great believer in good breeding and impeccable lineage. Why, both of us can trace our ancestors back two thousand years or more. And I can tell you that the rumours you may hear once you reach Dharanpore, regarding anticipated nuptials between the Prince and this unfortunate woman, have no basis whatsoever. I know Dickie as only a wife can, and I can tell you that he would have never married a working class woman so far beneath our station. After all, she was only a daughter of a Palace employee.'

'I understand your concern, Princess but please rest assured that neither my husband nor I will form any opinion regarding this case based on rumours and hearsay. More often than not, they tend to lead one away from the facts rather than taking one closer to the truth.'

'I am relieved to see that you are as intelligent and intuitive as people say you are.'

'Really, people say that about me? How extraordinary!' Rachel chuckled.

'My dear, your reputation precedes you. I believe you were the force behind catching the real culprits in two rather complicated cases.'

'Well, yes but between you and me, Princess, I rather fancy it was more of a coincidence, a concatenation of events than anything else.'

'Come now, you must not be modest if you have a gift. As my late father always told me, once can be a considered a coincidence, but having the same accident twice is carelessness. But of course that was in a different context but I am sure you get my drift.'

At that moment the maid came back with a tea tray and served them. Rachel and the Princess spent the next half an hour discussing the weather, books, theatre, fashion and several other topics that skilfully avoided anything to do with India or the case. Rachel realised that the Princess had subtly and successfully played her manipulative cards and she was impressed at how skilfully she had gone about it.

Chapter Seven

'So, the Princess quite categorically claims that while the Prince may have taken a passing fancy to Kitty, nothing on earth would have induced him to actually make an offer of marriage. Apparently Kitty was 'far below his station' for him to even entertain thoughts around matrimony. It certainly didn't stop him from paying her an inordinate amount of attention at the banquet, from what I can gather,' Rachel told Jeremy as they sat in the lounge enjoying a drink before dinner. She had just finished bringing him up to date with her meeting with the Princess and the contradictory narrative in Kitty's journal.

'Looks like she wants us to rule her out as suspect number one,' Jeremy said with a smile.

'Yes, I did think of that. After all, if the Prince had no intention of marrying Kitty, the Princess would have no obvious motive to get her out of the way.'

'Yes, but there could also be an element of truth in what she claims. These royal types do have a thing for lineage and breeding and that sort of thing and does it say anywhere in Kitty's journal that the Prince actually made a proposal of marriage?' Jeremy asked.

'Well, if it's there, I haven't got to that part yet. Although I don't think that all that guff about breeding would stop anyone from being with the person they truly love. Judging from the Colonel's grisly stories, it certainly didn't stop those other Maharajahs from marrying women below their station. Besides, Kitty wasn't a charwoman, you know. She was a smart, beautiful and respectable English girl who had the courage to fly planes for her country when it was at war. And I know that she could trace her ancestors back to about four generations at least, which is more than most people can these days. Daughter of a Palace employee indeed! I'm beginning to sense that there was something more than just a passing romance here. You ought to read the journal. Kitty is not as big a fool as the Colonel made her out to be. She seems to be as shocked with her own response towards the Prince as the next sane person.'

'You are quite the little romantic, aren't you?'

'All I am saying is that I don't think we should rule out Princess Uma's motives, just yet. Who knows to what extent she may have resented the idea of playing second fiddle to what she considered a potentially 'second rate, working class' Maharani, who had the affections of her husband in totality! She seems to be a ruthless type of woman who would easily kill someone without turning a hair if she felt her position in the Royal family was being threatened. '

'Charming! You've taken quite a shine to her, haven't you?' Jeremy asked with good natured sarcasm.

Rachel responded with her nose in the air, 'Well, if she wasn't such an unmitigated snob, I'd probably have liked her a little more.'

At that point, Colonel Riverton had walked up behind Rachel and asked, 'Who's an unmitigated snob? Sorry, didn't mean to eavesdrop but you were in full voice like a contralto at Verdi's!'

Jeremy explained, 'That's alright, Colonel. Rachel is just recovering from her meeting with the Princess Uma Devi, earlier in the day.'

'Ah! Seeing as there are no sharp objects about, I think I can safely say – I told you so!' He guffawed at Rachel, as he sat down.

Rachel spoke up, 'You have me there. Tell me Colonel, you seem to know these royals through and through. Do you think that if Kitty hadn't been murdered when she was, there was a chance that she would have ended up as the second Maharani?'

He answered carefully, 'I don't quite know what went on between those two. I know for sure that Kitty was head-over-heels in infatuation to the point where she couldn't think straight. But the Prince is an entirely different kettle of fish. He is after all the Crown Prince of a very large State and don't forget that these chaps are taught to cultivate diplomacy from infancy - all the genuine royals are. They've managed to raise it to an art form. You can get close to them but you never really know what's going on in their heads. You may think you know but then you realise that you know only what they want you to believe and know and that it's been very carefully planted in your head.'

Rachel said, 'That's rather well put. Let me re-phrase the question. What did the Prince lead you to believe and know regarding his intentions towards your daughter?'

'Please don't get me wrong, he never really said it in so many words, one can hardly expect that but what I gathered was the impression that he was going to marry Kitty once he could get his father – the Maharajah's approval.'

Rachel smiled triumphantly, 'See, Jeremy, what did I tell you?'

The Colonel piped up, 'It won't do any good to get excited about that, my dear as I know full well that what he gave me to believe may have simply been a mask for his real intentions, whatever those may have been. As I said, he holds his cards very close to his chest and I would have to be a magician to see the full hand.'

'Can you arrange a meeting with the Prince, for us?' Rachel asked.

'Certainly, but if you think you can go in all guns blazing, and ask him direct questions, you will be in for a serious disappointment, my dear. He is quite masterful at evading uncomfortable questions and he will not hesitate to politely put you in your place.'

'So what do you suggest we do?' Rachel asked, slightly miffed that the Colonel had caught her drift so quickly.

'For now, nothing. Just bide your time. Enjoy the voyage and all the interesting views it has to offer. Catch up on your reading. Relax. Your real work will start only once you get to Dharanpore. And then pardon me, if I sound patronizing but I do mean well and believe me, when I say that I want you to succeed more than anyone else - if you are as good as Harrow says you are, you will have plenty to do. I have kept all the evidence intact and Kitty's room in the Palace, along with all her things, is kept locked, and is exactly how she left it. There are only two keys, one is with me and one is with a very trustworthy amah ...er that's the Indian word for a maid by the way, who supervises the room being aired and cleaned once a week.'

Rachel sighed but she didn't give up. 'You could at least give us a brief on how and when Kitty was killed and run us through the list of suspects, or does that also have to wait until we reach Dharanpore?'

'Well, my dear, I could give you the skeletal information if you think it will help. To begin with, she was found dead by some servants in a marble folly on the grounds. It's not exactly a folly but how can I describe it? I suppose, it's more like a raised platform with a marble dome held up by carved marble pillars, open to all four sides. It's a place where musicians and dancers usually perform to entertain royal guests.'

'Something like an Indian version of a stage?'

'You could say that.'

'When was she found?'

'In the early morning hours when Angela raised the alarm saying that Kitty's bed hadn't been slept in and that she was worried. She had popped her head in the night before but hadn't thought anything of it when she didn't find Kitty in her room. Kitty kept late hours and she did spend a great deal of time in the Prince's company wandering about the grounds after dinner. But something had set off Angela's sixth sense and she woke up earlier than usual. The first thing she did that morning was to check if Kitty was in her bed and then raised the alarm.'

'I see, and how was she killed?'

'That is where this case takes a devilish twist. You see, we still have no idea how Kitty was killed.'

'That does sound rather strange,' Rachel said, as she sat up from her slightly reclining position.

'It does, doesn't it? Till date no one has been able to figure out what the murder weapon was. You see, her mouth was full of blood. Initially we thought that she had been made to drink something corrosive but eventually the doctor, who did the autopsy, informed us that there was a tiny hole in her upper palate, the roof of the mouth. And that it was made by something metallic like a thin curved metal rod or a large fishing hook. Owing to the tiny size of the hole, we managed to rule out fire arms, knives, daggers and poison.'

'And the weapon was not conclusively identified as a metal rod or a fish hook?' Jeremy asked, his interest piqued.

'No, we did round up anything that could have caused a wound like that but the Doctor rejected them all – they were either too big or too small.'

Rachel asked, 'Could it have been a sting or a bite made by some reptile like a snake or a small poisonous animal?'

'Apparently not, as there was a slight trace of some metallic residue on the palate but he couldn't say for sure because the blood flowing down from the brain into the mouth had literally washed it away. And he had a rather primitive microscope to work with. He also did a blood analysis that positively ruled out any form of poison – reptilian or otherwise. So it could not have been a snake bite or a sting. Besides, he did tell us that this weapon, whatever it was, had entered the brain and had killed her instantly. I can hardly see a snake or an animal doing that.'

Jeremy said, 'No, I quite agree, the angle of the wound would be all wrong.'

'That's right Jeremy. You've hit the nail on the head although that's possibly the worst analogy I could've used under the circumstances. Let's say, even something like a porcupine quill would be impossible to insert all the way up to the brain because you would quite literally have to open the mouth wide enough to have it standing vertically within the mouth and then push from under the chin. And there was no laceration on the chin or the lower jaw. Which is why the Doctor suggested a thin curved hook like weapon.'

Rachel asked, 'What about a curved metal wire? Or something made from a clothes hanger?'

'Not the right size as the wound and it would require a tremendous amount of thrust to pass into the brain. Ever tried killing anyone with a clothes hanger? Trust me, we looked into all existing possibilities and nothing matched. And then removing it would have caused the membranes of the palate to turn outwards but the Doctor said that is what puzzled him the most. He said that even if it were a fish hook like thing, the very act of removing it from the mouth would have caused the palate to turn outwards. Whatever it was, would have to be pulled out from the other end at the top of the skull.'

'And was there a laceration on the skull?' Jeremy asked.

'Yes. There was a tiny hole at the top of the skull right in line with the hole on the roof of the mouth or palate, which would once again point to something straight being used but you wouldn't be able to get in a rod of that length to fit in the mouth in the first place to push it up and the darndest thing is that it could not have been the other way round since all the membranes were flattened in the opposite direction.'

'So what you are saying is that it could not have been pushed in from the top and then pulled out?'

'No, the Doctor quite conclusively explained that the membranes would have shown the signs of having being pushed both ways. So no, whatever it was entered the palate, made its way up straight and left from the top of the head. He said it was a clean wound.'

'Well I'll be dashed!' Jeremy was puzzled.

'We all were. Not to mention completely baffled as well. And there was something else – a set of muddy footprints going to and fro from where her body lay, made by bare feet which points to a native and it was not made by the servants who found her. The chaps who found her were wearing juttees or handmade Indian shoes made from thick cloth on their feet. There were no other footprints around Kitty's body.'

Jeremy said, 'But then those could have been made by some native to who had seen something and gone near the body only to be scared away when he found her dead, thinking he would be blamed. Judging by the bizarre murder weapon used, one can only assume that we are up against a Machiavellian mind and such a person would hardly leave a clear set of footprints. '

Rachel asked, 'What was the time of death?'

'Between one and three am. Kitty was found in the evening dress she had worn at dinner with the Prince but the jewelled necklace with the star ruby – the Pride of Dharanpore was missing and there were some marks on her neck that showed that the person who took it off may have struggled to do so.'

'So do you suspect that she was killed and the real motive was robbery?'

'It could be – but then it would have been far easier to have just rendered her unconscious and taken the thing. But the necklace was very valuable. It was designed by Cartier's and the star ruby on it alone, was insured for a million pounds.'

Rachel gasped, 'People have been murdered for a lot less, Colonel.'

'I know but something about the weapon used and the devilishness of the crime leads me to suspect that it was a crime perpetrated by someone who must have hated her with a vengeance.'

Jeremy asked, 'Suspects?'

'That's the tricky thing. Since we had no clue as to what the murder weapon was, we also had no clue as to who could have committed the crime. So there really are no true suspects. All I can give you is a list of people who may have had some motive and in all fairness; I come into that equation as well, along with the others present in the Palace at the time. Though, I hardly think my motive of a disapproving father is strong enough to have killed my own daughter in cold blood with an ingenious weapon that was designed to baffle.'

Rachel said nothing for a few moments as she put her hand on his.

Then she said in a quiet voice, 'Recounting all this must be so difficult for you.'

'Well, it has to be done, if we are to get to the bottom of this. Oh, I've grieved over Kitty's death and I think all I want now, is for her to rest in peace and give her the justice that she deserves. Falling in love with someone, however unsuitable or wearing a necklace, however valuable is not reason enough to be killed so ruthlessly.'

Chapter Eight

RMS Arundel docked at Port Said, in Egypt. They had finally reached the mouth of the Suez Canal. This was her last refuelling stop before making the tail end of the journey to the final port of call - Bombay.

Rachel stood on the deck and listened attentively as the Colonel spoke of the significance of Port Said. 'Port Said is considered to be the meeting point between the West and East. From here on, according to Maritime Charts, we will technically be sailing in the East. You may have noticed that all the ship's officers have changed into their white uniforms. And shortly they will be erecting double awnings over the decks.'

Rachel replied, 'Yes, I did notice the change in uniforms. And I gather from the steward that today is also 'baggage day' when all the luggage containing our hot weather clothes will be brought up from the hold and exchanged for that marked 'cabin.'

'Yes. By the time we all go ashore and come back on board, we will have the new set of luggage in our cabins.'

'When can we go ashore?'

'Hopefully, in an hour's time and then I shall escort you both to Simon Artz, where you can follow the age old ritual of travellers to India, by picking up authentic solar topis and anything else you fancy that you may need in a hot climate. I suggest a lace parasol – they had a wonderful collection when I last visited. I got one each for Dorothea and Angela.'

The Princess joined them on the deck along with other members of the royal entourage. She addressed the Colonel, 'Good morning, Colonel. When you go ashore, could you kindly drop in at Simon Artz and get some toys for the children - a model airplane set for Prince Aditya and a doll's set for Princess Padma?'

'Certainly, Princess,' Colonel replied.

Rachel spoke, 'Does that mean you will not be coming ashore with us, Princess?'

'I would have loved to, but unfortunately my husband is a bit under the weather and I need to be by his side.'

'I am sorry to hear that. Is it seasickness?'

'No, he seems to have had something at dinner that didn't agree with him. The ship's doctor has given him some pills and advised rest.'

'Oh, dear, please do wish him a speedy recovery from our end.'

'Thank you, Lady Markham. I shall.'

II

By tea time Jeremy and Rachel had had their fill of sightseeing and shopping and had returned to the ship with their packages from Simon Artz. Apart from the solar topis, they had each bought a pair of lightweight walking shoes designed for tropical weather. Rachel had passed the pretty parasol display and decided that she wanted one of those new fangled Polaroid Land cameras instead. They had just been released earlier in the year and Rachel thought it was magical how it churned out pictures instantly and all one had to do was snap the shutter, turn a knob and wait for sixty seconds! The salesman informed her that once the print came out all one had to do was peel off the exposed negative from the paper and you would have a developed picture in your hands! No more dark rooms and the interminable wait to get a dry picture. Jeremy had followed suit and bought a pair of high end binoculars.

Excited with her new camera, the first picture she took was one of Colonel Riverton and Jeremy standing side-by-side on the street in front of Simon Artz and then one of RMS Arundel at anchor. After a spot of tea onboard with Jeremy and Colonel Riverton, she excused herself from the table and made her way towards the upper deck to take a few shots of the picturesque Port Said Harbour, from the ship's deck, while the light lasted.

As she climbed the steps, there was a young Indian gentleman coming down. He looked familiar and as he reached her, he tipped his hat at her and said, 'Good evening, Lady Markham. Would you happen to know if

Colonel Riverton is back on board? The Princess would like a word with him.'

'Yes, we came back together. You will find him in the dining hall having tea with my husband.'

'Thank you, ma'am,' he said, as he crossed her.

Rachel turned and addressed him, 'You are welcome... er, I'm sorry, but I don't know your name, we haven't been introduced.'

'My apologies. I ought to have introduced myself. I am Sushanto Bose, Prince Ravindra Richard Dharan's ADC.'

'Oh, of course. I saw you when you boarded the ship. You were with the Prince.'

'That's right.'

'I was sorry to hear that the Prince was unwell this morning. I hope he's feeling better now.'

'I'm afraid, he's taken a turn for the worse. The Princess is very worried. If you'll excuse me, I must get Colonel Riverton and then try and locate the ship's doctor,' he said with a worried expression as he left.

Rachel wondered if she ought to look in on the Royal couple and offer her assistance but then decided that it would make more sense to do so after the doctor had paid them a visit. Besides, judging from the size of their entourage, the Princess probably had too many people to assist her already.

III

Later that evening, Colonel Riverton joined Jeremy and Rachel at the dinner table. He was late and had missed the first course. He looked tired as he sat down.

'How is the Prince?' Rachel asked.

'Quite ill. The doctor says he has a severe case of food poisoning; however, the Princess is not happy with that explanation. She seems to think that it's a different kind of poisoning altogether. When she asked him to check for other poisons, the doctor quite categorically told her that there was no need for that since the Prince himself had admitted to imbibing a large quantity of escargot the night before.'

'I gather that didn't convince her.'

'No, it did not. And to make matters worse, she then proceeded to get quite hysterical and asked him where he had gotten his medical degree from, which did not help the situation. The doctor was livid and told her to leave the stateroom so he could treat the patient in peace. Thank goodness, I was there to prevent her from doing him an injury! It took all my tact and the better part of the past hour to soothe her royal ruffled feathers. The things one has to do for a living!'

Rachel smiled. 'Tsk, tsk, Colonel, you do have my sympathies. You've had quite an evening. But tell me, why does the Princess think that he's been poisoned? Does she suspect he has enemies onboard?'

'Not to my knowledge but then one never knows. His younger brother is on board and there was an unfortunate shooting incident last year, when the younger Prince - Yuvraj Dharan had accidentally shot his brother, while they were both out, alone on Shikaar... er that's the Indian word for hunting.'

'Really? How can you accidentally shoot a person when you are out shooting birds and animals?'

'Oh, it happens when you are operating under heavy foliage. It was Prince Dickie's fault really. He had gone ahead of his brother and had dismounted from his horse to avoid startling the 'Sambar' - the deer, they were stalking. His brother hadn't seen him dismount. And when he saw some bushes rustle ahead, he thought the animal had taken shelter there and took a shot at it. Luckily, he only winged the Prince. But I am quite sure it was an accident because Yuvraj was aghast at what he had done and had ridden home hard with the unconscious Prince on his saddle. His quick thinking and swift action is what saved the Prince's life that day. But I suppose that incident could have triggered a sense of insecurity in the Princess. Widows, even royal ones, have a hard time in India and for the most part, lead powerless lives.'

The next few days proved that the ship's doctor had been right and the Princess' fears had indeed been unfounded, as the Prince made a quick recovery under the doctor's medical supervision and his strict administration of the Prince's diet. By the time they had reached Bombay port, he had completely recovered.

Chapter Nine

The royal chartered flight had flown twenty two members of the Royal entourage including Jeremy and Rachel from Bombay to Dharanpore air field. The others were to follow by rail. Far from the rigours of the train journey, which Kitty had described in detail, the comfortable air-conditioned flight had taken a mere three hours to reach its destination. So far, India had lived up to her promise of delivering unexpected surprises and had proved to be an antithesis of every preconceived notion Rachel had entertained in her mind about the country. Even the drive from the airfield to the Dharanpore Palace was marked with luxury and style that Rachel despite her lineage, had never previously experienced. A fleet of waiting Rolls-Royces had whisked them off to a royal welcome at the Palace itself.

Nothing had prepared her for her first glimpse of Dharanpore Palace, not even Kitty's journal which was still lying half read in her travel satchel. It was a magnificent structure made of golden sandstone and designed on similar lines of the Palace at Versailles. As they drove past the acres of lush lawns, towards the main entrance, every glittering window in the edifice seemed to reflect the molten gold of the evening Sun in a dazzling display to greet them. Rachel was enchanted.

The gardens surrounding the vast lawns were dotted with well maintained flower beds and fruit trees and Rachel thought she spotted a large exotic bird in the distance near an enormous ornate water fountain. Colonel Riverton explained that it was a peacock – one of the many that roamed the gardens and he chuckled as he informed her that they sometimes terrorised the gardeners by giving chase, especially if they were inadvertently disturbed during mating season.

Colonel Riverton smiled and asked, 'Not what you expected, is it?'

Rachel responded, 'I didn't know what I expected but certainly not something on quite so grand a scale! It looks bigger than Buckingham Palace.'

Riverton responded, 'Now that you mention it I must share with you an anecdote of when the Prince of Idar, Rajendrasingh visited England for the first time, he was so shocked and disappointed by the size of Buckingham Palace that he is said to have famously remarked to his English companions – 'I could point out ten, if not twenty Palaces in India, such as the Palace of the Maharajah of Jodhpur or the Palaces of the Maharajah of Mysore before which the Queen's Palace pales by comparison.' At the time, his remark made waves in royal circles for days and although tactless, it was certainly true. Indian Palaces are built, in most part, on such a massive scale that unless one visits, it is not easy to comprehend. What you've seen so far is just the front facade, which is one fifth of the entire Palace structure. The grounds extend for miles in all directions. And Dharanpore has a relatively mid-sized Palace. The Palaces up north are of course are much larger and their forts contain entire cities within. Of course, I've lived here for twenty five odd years so it's easy for me to forget how overwhelming it can all be, for new visitors.'

They were given a traditional Indian welcome with garlands and sweetmeats and shown up to their rooms by the Palace staff. Jeremy and Rachel were in the 'European wing' on the first floor and here at least, Rachel knew what to expect from Kitty's descriptive writing. She was not disappointed. Jeremy and she had been allocated a suite of rooms with connecting doors and a luxurious shared bath. Both rooms had high ceilings and hers had three large windows overlooking the beautiful back garden that extended onto the woods at the deep end. She could see the marble folly on the grounds from where she stood.

Rachel noticed there was a study table and chair facing the middle window. She walked towards it and put her satchel on the chair. Looking about her, she saw that next to the study table, in front of the third window, there were two comfortable silk covered arm chairs placed around a low marble topped table. She walked about the room and noticed that the walls had carefully selected photographs, paintings and lithographs that depicted not only the members of the royal family – past and present, but also the history and natural beauty of Dharanpore. She was impressed.

The furniture was made from exquisitely carved Burma teak and the soft furnishings were in contrasting stripes of burgundy and cream silk. At the center of the room, there was a queen sized four poster bed with matching burgundy silk drapes and a cushioned ottoman at its foot. A cream silk covered settee with burgundy cushions, was placed against the left wall, next to the entrance. A large ornate three-door wardrobe stood facing the bed. There were two doors on either side of the wardrobe – one, she knew connected to Jeremy's room. He had come in a few minutes earlier to ask her if she wanted to join him for a small walk around the grounds. She had declined in favour of a bath and some rest.

The other door, she soon discovered opened into her private dressing area with a full length mirror, a dressing table and stool, a wooden clothes stand and a small settee. There was also another door in the dressing area that connected to the bath. She opened it to find that the amah was already running a bath for her. The smell of lavender bath salts hung heavy in the air and had a calming effect on her tired mind and body. She smiled and shook her head as the amah asked if she needed anything else before leaving. She thanked her and then peeling off her travel worn clothes, she sank into the bath to relax. As the foam began to dissipate she realised that she was surround by rose petals. I could get used to this, she thought to herself as she closed her eyes and inhaled the luxury of it all.

By the time she had bathed and rested, it was time to dress for dinner. They were to dine with the Prince and Princess in their private dining room. Rachel chose to dress in a sleeveless white ankle length sheath accentuated only with a set of pearl earrings. She put on minimal makeup and swept up her overgrown auburn curls into a top knot. She added a pearl hair pin on one side as a finishing touch. She glanced at herself in the mirror in approval and noticed that she had lost weight on the voyage. Her cheekbones were more prominent, her arms were beautifully tanned and her neck looked slender and delicate. Jeremy came in to the dressing room and gave a low whistle.

'You look stunning, darling. How did you manage a transformation like this in three hours?'

'I am going to take that as a compliment, Jeremy Richards. Although it would have been better, had you stopped at the stunning part.'

'Well darling, you enter this room as yourself and come out looking like the Queen of Sheba, what is a man supposed to say?'

'Yet another compliment. You seem to be in good voice tonight, darling. Now, will you be so kind, as to escort the Queen of Sheba to dinner. She's starving and hoping for an eight course meal.'

'I can't promise you an eight course meal, Your Highness, but your every other wish is my command. Pray, take my arm.'

Chapter Ten

The Khidmatgar assigned to them – Teji Singh was a tall young man in a splendid uniform that included a scarlet turban and a cummerbund. He was waiting in the main hall to escort them to the private dining room. They walked through a labyrinth of hallways and staircases till they reached a central courtyard. From there, they walked through a latticed, trellis covered corridor that led to large double doors with an armed sentry on either side. As they approached, the sentries saluted and opened the doors to let them in. They found themselves in a plush solarium like space that had tropical plants, water fountains, wrought iron garden furniture and a large parrot in a gilded cage who squawked, 'Hazir hai! Hazir hai!'

Just as Rachel wondered what that meant, the Khidmatgar crossed the solarium and opened yet another set of doors, turned sideways to let them pass and announced loudly into the room, 'Richards saab hazir hai! Memsaab hazir hai!'

Colonel Riverton came out of a doorway to greet them and told the Khidmatgar, 'Thank you, Teji Singh. You can go now. Aap jaa sakte hai. I will escort them from here.'

The Khidmatgar gave a curt nod, salaamed and left.

'Come, my dears. Let me introduce you to everyone,' he said, as they followed him into a glittering living room strewn with gilded Louis XIV furniture, breathtaking Persian carpets and rare artefacts set atop glistening carved tables. Rachel fancied she saw a Faberge egg on one of them. Genuine masters, portraits of royal ancestors along with hunting trophies of tigers, deer and bison stared down at them from the walls. There was a bar at the other end of the room and Rachel saw another Indian couple were present apart from the Prince and Princess.

The Princess looked beautiful in a turquoise blue chiffon sari. Rachel noticed that she was wearing a stunning emerald necklace around her milky throat and exquisite emerald teardrops hung from her ears. She came forward to welcome them with a smile, 'Rachel, Jeremy, I hope you've settled in comfortably. Come and say hello to my husband and brother-in-law. '

'You've met my husband, Prince Ravindra and this is his younger brother – Prince Yuvraj Dharan,' then with a wave of her hand towards the other young lady in a pink sari, she said, 'And this is Princess Tara, my sister-in-law, Yuvraj's wife.'

The men shook hands as introductions were made and then they headed to the bar stools while the ladies walked towards the sofas. Princess Tara smiled and as they made themselves comfortable on the sofas and said to Rachel, 'I have heard a lot about you from Princess Uma and I'm very pleased to finally meet you, Rachel. I do love your dress.'

'Thank you and likewise, Princess – I think your sari is the most exquisite dress I've ever seen,' Rachel said with a smile.

They were offered white wine and hors d'oeuvres by a uniformed attendant wearing white gloves.

Princess Uma spoke, 'Rachel, I have asked some of our staff to join us for dinner. People who have been with us for three years or more. I thought it would help break the ice and help you carry out your investigations as discreetly as possible. After all we don't want everyone running scared. Except for Colonel Riverton and the family members present at the moment, no one else is wise to the real reason behind your visit as yet, and we would like to keep it that way.'

'That was very thoughtful of you, Princess. And you are right. There is no point in alarming anyone.'

The doors opened and the sentry announced, 'Doctor Saunders, hazir hai!'

Jeremy and Colonel Riverton came towards Rachel, and the Colonel said, 'I'd like you to meet Dr. Saunders – the Royal Physician. Remember, we spoke about him on the ship when I described Kitty's... er... the incident.'

'Ah, yes,' she said, as she got up to meet the doctor. She thought to herself, so he is the one who performed the autopsy that yielded such baffling results. Dr. Saunders was about fifty-five. He had a pleasant weather beaten face, white hair and moustaches and clear blue eyes. Like the other men, he too was dressed in a dinner jacket although his looked a bit crumpled, as if it had been taken out of a trunk in a hurry for this occasion and he hadn't bothered to have it pressed.

Colonel Riverton introduced them, 'Dr. Saunders, this is Jeremy Richards and this lovely young lady is his wife, Rachel.'

Dr. Saunders gave them a wide smile and said in a loud voice, 'Very pleased to meet you both. The Colonel has informed me that you are here to investigate his daughter's death. About time too. Terrible business. In all my years in India, I've never seen anything like it.'

The Princess looked alarmed and said, 'Dr. Saunders! Please! I just finished informing Rachel that we don't want the real reason for their visit, bandied about.'

'Well, alright. But I can't see how they can go about their investigations without people knowing what they're here for, Princess. If I were you, I'd inform everybody and let them deal with it. Like taking plaster off a wound, if you have to do it, you might as well do it quickly.'

'Yes I'm sure you would have, Doctor, but you are not me. And I would infinitely prefer it my way, thank you very much,' the Princess said with thinly veiled impatience.

'Up to you, Princess, but all of us know that it's dashed hard to keep anything a secret in a place like this. Starting with the servants, word gets around and anyhow, they probably know already. But if you want me to keep mum about it, I will.'

'Thank you, yes. Keeping mum, will do quite nicely, for the time being.'

The doors opened once more and the sentry announced, 'Missy Rosie, hazir hai!'

A chubby young white woman with shingled blond hair, entered. She was wearing a printed cotton frock and looked awkwardly about her as though she was not used to being in such a situation.

The Princess came to her rescue. 'Come in, Rosie and join us. Are the children asleep?'

Rosie looked relieved as she walked towards the ladies and answered, 'Yes, Princess. All tucked in. The amah's with them in the nursery. They have had a long day and were all tired out, so I gave them dinner at seven thirty and they are fast asleep now.'

'That's good. I shall check in on them afterwards. Come and meet Lady Rachel Markham. Lady Markham, this is our nanny - Miss Rosie Dent. I have asked her to join us for dinner. I think she will be of immense help in showing you around the grounds in the coming days. Apart from being a nanny, Rosie takes quite an interest in gardening. Under her supervision, we've managed to plant an orchid nursery as well.'

Rosie gave a shy smile and said in a soft voice, 'I can show you about, tomorrow, Lady Markham. We are quite proud of the orchid nursery, ma'am. Even the royal children are learning ever so much and are such gardening enthusiasts now.'

Rachel replied gently, 'That sounds delightful. I would really appreciate that and perhaps take some gardening tips from you, for my own garden back in England. Please do take a seat.'

Rachel was amused at how adeptly the Princess had brought in the 'Lady Markham' bit while introducing her to the nanny. Rosie smiled and sat down on a sofa at a little distance from them. She was definitely feeling out of place. Rachel also noticed that while the uniformed bearer offered her some hors d'oeuvres, he did not offer her any wine.

Soon a few more people came in. Jeremy and Rachel were introduced to Elliot Wilkins, a thin lipped, pale faced, bespectacled young man who was tutor to the royal children and had been in Dharanpore Palace for four years. He had walked in with Prince Dickie's ADC – Sushanto Bose, whom Rachel had already met on the voyage.

The last person to arrive was Miss Martha – a middle aged lady who was the Governess to the royal children. She was dressed in a stiff high necked black dress with a white lace collar and reminded Rachel of the nuns at her own school. She looked just as strict and unbending as they had.

Soon after that dinner was announced. Rachel was delighted to find that she was seated near Prince Dickie who was at the head of the table. She had wanted the opportunity to talk to him.

While she found that the dinner conversation was stilted, the food was excellent. Prince Dickie turned out to be a taciturn man who did not speak unless spoken to. But as Rachel found out, he did have a sense of humour.

'I must congratulate you on your chef, Your Highness. The food is simply delicious.'

'Thank you. I found our chef - Alberto while I was travelling through Spain. We had stopped at an Inn near Seville after a long journey, and I was amazed at the food we were served there. I asked to meet the chef and made an 'on-the-spot-offer', so to speak. The upshot was he agreed and we've been putting on weight ever since.'

Rachel laughed and said, 'You have such an enormous home, Your Highness, I am sure you can keep off any amount of weight by just walking from one end of your house to the other. And after tasting Chef Alberto's cooking, I think I had better start taking some exercise on your extensive grounds myself, while I am here.'

'If that doesn't work, let me know. You could walk Sheba every night after dinner. She'll make sure you get enough exercise and more. She's quite feisty.'

Rachel almost choked on her dessert, 'Oh, how nice. You have a doggy called Sheba! It's one of my husband's favourite names, isn't it, Jeremy?' She asked him across the table as Jeremy, who had heard their conversation, was trying to control his mirth. He nodded his head meaningfully.

The Prince offered, 'She's not much of a doggy, er... never mind. I think I'll just surprise you. Do you feel up to going for a small walk after dinner?'

'Why not? Jeremy, are you up for a little walk?'

'Certainly, though I doubt I'll be able to keep up with Sheba after all the food I seem to have ingested,' he said laughingly, as Rachel narrowed her eyes at him and his double entendre.

Chapter Eleven

Jeremy and Rachel waited alongside with the Prince as he dispatched one of his sentries to bring Sheba out for a walk. They were rendered speechless for a moment when Sheba finally made an appearance. She was a full sized leopard with a diamond studded collar held on a thick chain. As she neared them, she hissed at Rachel, who in turn, ducked behind Jeremy.

The Prince commanded, 'Down, Sheba! Behave yourself.' Then turning to look at Rachel, he said gently, 'Don't worry, she's really quite nice, once you get to know her. Like most women, she has a jealous streak and tends to get a bit suspicious around other women.' The Prince smiled at Rachel and petted the leopard to reassure her. The leopard seemed to enjoy it and rubbed herself against the Prince.

'See?'

Jeremy reached out and stroked Sheba's luxurious golden fur and said in admiration, 'You are a big, beautiful girl, aren't you?'

Sheba rubbed herself against Jeremy and Rachel found the courage to pet her as well. Sheba began enjoying all the attention and came closer to inspect Rachel.

Rachel spoke in a soft voice, 'You needn't be jealous of me, Sheba. You really are gorgeous.' The leopard looked at her with topaz eyes and as if she understood what Rachel had said, she started licking her hand. Her tongue felt like sand paper.

'Shall we?' The Prince asked, as he made a move to start walking the leopard.

'Seriously? You walk her on your own, without her keeper?'

'I've brought her up since she was a cub. We had shot a female leopard on Shikaar a few years ago. When we reached the carcass we found this little one desperately clambering all over her dead mother, trying to suckle. I brought her back to the Palace and she's been with us ever since. She's really quite domesticated. Even the children enjoy playing with her, once in a while, though Uma gets nervous everytime they do.'

Rachel responded, 'I don't blame her. One hears stories. They say wild cats can never be completely harmless or domesticated and that they can be quite unpredictable.'

'I can't speak for other wild cats but this one is like a pet, an affectionate little cat. Aren't you, Sheba? Except for a few odd incidents she has led a completely blameless life, haven't you, darling?' He said, cooing to the leopard.

'What kind of incidents?' Jeremy asked.

'Nothing serious, sometimes she likes to wrestle people to the ground just for the fun of it.'

'I can see how that could alarm an unsuspecting visitor to the Palace,' Rachel said laughingly.

The Prince spoke. 'Thing is, when she was a cub, she used to be let loose in the back garden at night. It's my private walled garden so I didn't think there would be any harm in it. Unfortunately she got used to her freedom and as she got older I had to start caging her. She began showing a certain amount of resentment at being caged.'

'I suppose I would too, if I were in her place,' Rachel said with a grimace.

'I had no choice. There were times when we had a large number of guests staying over at the Palace and I could not allow her to roam about freely, even at night. She's not dangerous but unsuspecting guests don't know that. I was more concerned for her well being than anything else. People sometimes stroll about in the dead of the night. I didn't want her to playfully jump on some royal guest and have them whip out a pistol and shoot her!'

Jeremy said, 'I agree. But how many close encounters led you to start caging her.'

'Not many, just one or two. She once pounced on a new amah in my wife's employ. That was about two years ago. If you ask me, the woman had no business to be in the back garden, at that time in the night, in the first place. The old retainers know better than to roam about here at night.'

Rachel noticed that their walk had led them towards the marble folly. The marble dome shone silver under the moonlight and it looked much larger up close. Its interior was in complete darkness beyond the pillars. This was where Kitty's body had been found two years ago. Rachel gave an involuntary shudder as if someone had just walked over her bones.

Something compelled her to broach the subject of the Prince's relationship with Kitty. She remembered Colonel Riverton's warning against doing precisely that but threw caution to the winds.

'Your Highness, I am going ask you a personal question and I hope that you will not take offence and answer it in the right spirit.'

'Fire away.'

'What was the nature of your relationship with Kitty Riverton?'

'You want to know if all the rumours you have heard are true – that Miss Riverton and I were close friends?'

'Well, not quite. I already know that you both formed a very close friendship. I just wondered if there was something more.'

'I will answer that if you can convince me that it has a bearing on your investigation.'

'Our entire investigation hinges on it, Your Highness. For the simple reason that she was killed by someone who hated her beyond reason and...'

Before she could finish, he answered with a sad smile, 'Well then, you can rule me out. I certainly didn't. Kitty was a remarkable woman and I admired her strength and courage enormously. Did you know she flew planes during the war?'

'Yes, but that doesn't really answer my question,' Rachel said softly with a smile. She realised that she was being sidetracked and she wasn't about to give up. She played her next hand boldly. 'Were you lovers?' She asked him casually.

He answered in an even tone. 'How does it make any difference after all this time, if we were lovers or not? Even if we were, you know full well that nothing came of it. The question you ought to be asking me is whether or not I had anything to do with her death and I can tell you quite categorically that I did not.'

Rachel realised that she had played her hand and lost. She backed down gracefully. The Prince had sidestepped the issue with the diplomatic skills that the Colonel had credited him with.

He then turned to Jeremy and completely changed the subject, 'Would you care to walk Sheba?'

When Jeremy responded in the affirmative, the Prince handed Sheba's chain to him and explained how to keep her in control whilst giving her enough freedom.

Jeremy asked the Prince, 'You mentioned Sheba had attacked one or two people. Who was the second person?'

'The second person was a guest who had stayed back after the festivities were over. Arthur Blackwell. You probably know him. He's married to Colonel Riverton's younger daughter – Angela?'

Jeremy responded as he struggled to keep the powerful leopard under control, 'I've heard of him from the Colonel, of course, but we've never met. And two years ago, you say? That is interesting. When was this exactly?'

'About a few days after the fateful night Kitty Riverton was found dead here,' he said referring to the marble folly with a wave of his hand. 'Come, let's head back,' he said casually, as he held out his hand and Jeremy gratefully handed Sheba's heavy chain back to the Prince. The moment the chain was back in the Prince's hand, Sheba stopped straining at it.

Rachel spoke, 'Tell me, was Sheba caged the night Kitty was killed?'

'Come to think of it, I don't think so. Kitty was killed exactly a week after the royal banquet had ended. Most of the guests had left by then, so Sheba must've been let out. But if you are trying to suggest that she had anything to do with what happened to Kitty, you are mistaken. She would never harm Kitty. Sheba loved Kitty from their very first meeting. Kitty was the only other person apart from me, who could fearlessly take Sheba out on her nightly walks.

Jeremy said, 'That was very courageous of her.'

'Yes. Kitty was that sort a person and more so, she was very good around animals and children. She knew how to handle them. She often joined in our walks and once or twice walked Sheba alone when I was busy. In fact, if my memory serves me right, I think she had taken Sheba out for a walk, the night she was killed.'

Rachel spoke, 'Really, that's very interesting. Though I can understand why you don't think Sheba had anything to do with Kitty's death. Dr. Saunders positively ruled out an animal attack in his autopsy. But if Sheba was let loose that night, she may have been in the vicinity and seen the person who did.'

The Prince's face was unfathomable as it was in shadows but she could sense his underlying amusement when he deadpanned back, 'Really? Now that is food for thought. I suggest you interrogate Sheba thoroughly.'

Rachel smiled but didn't say anything as they headed back to the Palace. *Perhaps, Sheba had already given her a clue,* she thought to herself. *What was interesting was that Sheba attacked Arthur Blackwell two nights after Kitty was killed.* It made her wonder why.

Meanwhile the object of their conversation and attention - Sheba walked along contentedly at the Prince's side. In Rachel's mind, the experience of seeing the handsome young Prince walking his regal leopard in the moonlight against the backdrop of a royal Palace, made a powerful impression of the wealth and power that surrounded the man. And glancing back at Jeremy, she noticed that walking a step behind them, he too seemed lost in admiration for both the Prince and his magnificent pet.

Chapter Twelve

After breakfast, Jeremy accompanied Colonel Riverton to Dr. Saunders' Hospital at Dharanpore, which stood a little distance away from the Palace. He had wanted to go through the autopsy report.

Rachel stayed back at the Palace and went to look for Nanny Rosie, in the hope that she could talk to the woman and hear her version of the events that had taken place two years ago, whilst looking about the gardens. Teji Singh escorted her to the nursery wing in the Palace on the ground floor. It had large French windows overlooking a flower garden. Nanny Rosie came forward to greet Rachel. She looked harried.

'Good morning, Lady Markham. I am sorry I couldn't come to you but the little princess is having one of her days and refusing to attend the school room. Miss Martha usually makes her go but she is unwell today.

Mr. Elliot is not going to like it,' the nanny said, sounding woebegone.

'Is that her? She looks a bit small for school room, surely?' Rachel asked, looking at a toddler of about two. An amah was following the baby around with a bowl and a spoon, trying to feed the child who in turn was giggling and moving away from her, every time she got close enough with the spoon. The baby was holding a large doll in a pink frock with golden ringlet curls, and stopped walking to observe Rachel.

'Oh, no, ma'am. That is Prince Aditya – the heir to the throne!' Nanny Rosie said, with pride in her voice, as the heir to the throne toddled backwards, lost his balance, fell on his bottom and started wailing lustily. The amah rushed to pick him up and comfort him.

Just then a girl of about six, wearing a blue pinafore came running like the wind into the room, through the open French windows. She ran in with a model airplane held high in one hand. She was pretty and was on the thinner side, had spindly legs, black shoulder length hair, big brown eyes and a great deal of energy. 'Whoosh, whoosh... see, Nanny Rosie – I am flying an airplane!' She said with a grin that displayed a few missing teeth. She stopped short as she noticed Rachel and asked curiously, 'Who are you?'

Nanny Rosie said, 'Princess Padma! Where *are* your manners? This is your mummy's friend - Lady Rachel Markham and she has come to visit us. And how do we greet our visitors?'

The child looked suitably admonished, looked down at her shoes and said, 'Good morning.'

Rachel said to her with a smile, 'And a very good morning to you, my dear. That is a very nice airplane you have there, Princess. Are you training to be a pilot?'

'Yes! And when I grow up I am going to fly real planes like Kitty!' The child answered with a bright smile. Usually, most grown-ups were bossy and always telling her to mind her manners. This grown-up seemed alright to her.

Rachel clapped her hands and said, 'How wonderful! Though, I daresay that doll your brother is holding is quite nice too, I thought your mummy bought that for you.'

'I hate dolls. They are so silly and boring. I gave mine to my brother. He likes them.'

'Oh?'

Nanny Rosie said conspiratorially, 'It's true, she does hate dolls. Takes their heads off and buries them in the garden!'

'That's because they don't look like me! They all have golden hair. And mummy says black hair is beautiful too and when I grow up I'm going to have lovely long black hair.'

'Your mummy is right! I think you are very pretty already,' Rachel said.

'I know!'

'Princess Padma!' Nanny admonished as Rachel laughed.

'Er...thank you Lady...er...,'the little Princess fumbled.

'Call me Rachel and you are welcome, my dear.'

'Now I'm going to fly planes, Rachel,' she said happily and then as an afterthought, she offered, 'Do you want to come and fly planes with me?'

'I would have loved to, Princess, but I hear that you ought to be in the school room. You do realise that if you miss your lessons, you can't be a pilot when you grow up?'

'Oh? Why not?'

'Because pilots have to study very hard and do well at their lessons and only then they get to be pilots. It's a well kept secret. Kitty worked hard at her lessons and that's how she became a real life pilot.'

'Really?' The child asked her with saucer like eyes.

'Really, it's true. Ask any pilot and they will tell you,' Rachel said with conviction in her voice.

'Can I fly planes after I finish school room?'

'Absolutely! Flying practice is equally important. You know what they say – practice makes perfect. But you must attend your school room and then fly your plane. That's the secret to becoming a really good pilot.'

'Alright I'll go. But lessons are boring.'

'Just a few hours, my dear and then you can fly to your heart's content, I promise!'

'Will you be there when I get back?'

'Certainly! Although I must admit, I'm not as good as you when it comes to flying planes.'

'That's alright. I'll teach you.'

'Then it's a pact! You go to the school room now and in the evening after you've had your tea, you could teach me to fly!'

'Yippee. I like you, Rachel,' the child said with a happy smile.

'I like you too, Princess. Now off you go for your lessons,' Rachel responded with a smile.

As the child left, Nanny Rosie looked at Rachel with admiration and said, 'If I may say so, you are very good with children, ma'am.'

'Thank you, Nanny. Now, I suppose you could show me about the gardens and your famous orchid nursery.'

'Of course. The amah will be putting the Prince down for a nap now, so we can go.'

They started with a walk through the main gardens where Rachel duly admired the fragrant flower beds of tuberoses and marigold and well arranged patches of bright bougainvillea, roses and crotons, as nanny Rosie explained how the cool weather which would set in by October would be perfect for growing chrysanthemums and amaryllis and that she had also planned flower beds with imported seeds of xenias, petunias, asters and dog flowers that would come into bloom by early November.

After a round of the beautifully laid formal gardens, Nanny Rosie took her to the private garden where they had walked Sheba the night before. A path led off to a grove of mimosa trees and from there they took a left and found themselves in a trellised enclosure that had different kinds of orchids growing on mossy wooden latticed walls. Rachel found herself in an enchanted space. The space was cooler as it was shielded from the Sun and had higher humidity as several water bodies had been created in stone urns that contained lotus and water hyacinths.

They walked about as Nanny pointed out various types of vibrantly coloured orchids - Moth orchids, large boat orchids, Dendrobium and her personal favourite – the Lady's slipper orchid. It looked like a dainty velvet slipper and Nanny Rosie gave one to Rachel saying that she could pin it on her hair later. Rachel thanked her for the tour and congratulated her on creating the most beautiful orchid nursery she had ever seen.

Chapter Thirteen

Nanny Rosie suggested they head back to the Palace but Rachel had other ideas. She told her that she wanted to spend some more time in the peaceful haven of the orchid nursery and asked the nanny, if she didn't mind giving her company for a little longer. Rosie said she had nothing much to do back at the nursery, so they sat on a cool stone bench in a corner and talked. Rachel asked about her life and Nanny Rosie told her how she came to be in India and in the employ of the royal household. They spoke of various things till Rachel subtly and gradually brought in the topic of Palace intrigues and then asked her casually about Kitty.

'Miss Kitty was such a nice young lady. Always polite and so beautifully dressed. Why, I've never seen such beautiful clothes. And she could carry them. She had an air about her, you know and I've always wondered why Her Highness, Princess Uma detested her so much. Even people like Miss Martha and the others hated her so. I liked her. She was always very kind to me.'

'Perhaps, it was because His Highness, Prince Dickie was so very fond of her,' Rachel suggested.

'Yes, he was fond of her. They spent a lot of time together while she was here. And the little Princess Padma loved her too. Miss Kitty was so good with her. Why, you saw for yourself how she practically hero worships her still. I do sometimes wonder at what would have happened had she not died so tragically.'

'She didn't die, Rosie. She was brutally murdered by someone who was present in the Palace, at the time. I am going to share a secret with you - my husband and I are here to find out who killed her. You may not be aware of this but Jeremy - my husband worked at Scotland Yard for years and I help him solve cases like this.'

'In all honesty, ma'am, it's not much of a secret. Mr. Elliot Wilkins told Miss Martha and she told me that the Prince had called in the big guns from England to solve Miss Kitty's murder. And when you arrived, we put two and two together. And Mr. Wilkins said that we were all suspects and that's why we were all so nervous at dinner last night.'

'I see. But you have no reason to be nervous. In fact we could use your help. You see, as you rightly observed, most people at the Palace were probably glad to be rid of Kitty's presence altogether. And I don't think they will be very keen on getting her the justice she deserves. It's clear to me that she didn't have very many supporters or friends here, which is why you are so important to our investigation.

We are going to find out who did it but we can't do that without your help. Will you help us?'

'Why, yes ma'am. Though, I don't see how. Nobody knows who killed her, least of all me. I am in the nursery wing most of the time and don't really mingle much with the royals or their guests. Last night was the first time they ever asked me to join them for dinner.'

'But surely you had been invited to the royal banquet that was held at the time?'

'Oh, yes ma'am but I had to leave early with Princess Padma who was only four at the time and I was asked to put her to bed by eight thirty as usual, by Miss Martha. She is very strict about the children's timings and such. I could have gone back and joined the others had the princess slept but the child was naturally very excited with all the festivities and wanted to stay up to see the fireworks, so I let her. I had my dinner brought to me on a tray and we watched the fireworks together from the nursery windows. They were beautiful.'

'I'm sure they were. Tell me, is there anything you remember about those weeks, in particular, in the days leading up to the night that Kitty was killed? Can you recall anything unusual?'

'There was so much happening. I remember that they all went on a royal tiger shoot. A few days later, I was with them on the day, the Prince and Miss Kitty took Princess Padma on a picnic by the lake. We had taken the gramophone with us and Miss Kitty made us all play musical cushions! It was such fun. I remember the weather was perfect, it was a glorious day and the little girl had a wonderful time.

And then a few days after the picnic, I was delighted to hear that the Prince was going to marry Miss Kitty! The rumour was that he had gifted her a fabulous necklace – the Pride of Dharanpore, as an engagement gift. There was no formal announcement but I saw her wearing it a few nights before she was killed. I remember she looked ever so beautiful. She wore it for the last night of festivities, most of the royal guests were to depart the next day. And I got to see the necklace for myself as she came into the nursery, just before the dinner started, to say goodnight to Princess Padma. But what struck me most was that the necklace, however fabulous paled in front of her dazzling beauty. She was always beautiful but that night she had this special glow about her and she was wearing a beautiful red silk dress to go with the ruby necklace. The effect was simply stunning.'

'I see,' Rachel said, lost in thought and then coming back she asked, 'And do you know if Princess Uma had heard this rumour, about their engagement I mean. I believe she was in the ladies' quarters - the zenana, at the time?'

'Yes, I suppose she must have. The whole Palace was abuzz with the news and there was a lot of speculation amongst the staff.'

'She must have been quite livid.'

'Well, perhaps, I don't know that for sure but I don't see why. After all, I've heard that it is perfectly normal for an Indian Prince to have more than one wife. I mean, his own father, the Maharajah Paramjit Dharan has four!'

'Yes but I'm sure they were all arranged matches with high caste Hindu ladies from other Indian royal families.'

'I never thought of that. But come to think of it, that is true.'

'Rosie, please think back and tell me if you saw anything that seemed strange or suspicious around that time.'

'I can't think of anything at the moment, oh wait! There was that strange incident with Miss Kitty's amah, a few nights before she got killed.'

'What incident?'

'Why, the amah got attacked by that leopard! I remember wondering at the time what she was doing there in the middle of the night.'

'Did the amah tell anyone why she was there?'

'I believe, she said she was going to the zenana.'

'And you think there was something strange in that? Maybe she was just going back to her room to sleep.'

'That's the thing, you see. The servants who are assigned to the European guests have rooms in the servant's quarters near the European wing, so that they can take care of the guests and be on call, so to speak. Every room in that wing has a bell pull that rings in the servant's quarters. So the amah would have had quarters in the European wing, seeing as she was assigned to Miss Kitty. I don't see why she had to go to the zenana so late in the night.'

'That is very interesting, indeed. I didn't know that,' Rachel said, digesting this new piece of information. She also realised that while the Prince had mentioned that the amah had no business being there, he had conveniently misled them to believe that it had been his wife's amah.

On second thoughts, she realised that he had used the words – 'a new amah in my wife's employ'.

She realised that Colonel Riverton had been right all along, about him being able to carefully plant ideas in one's head! She wondered if the Prince had deliberately wanted them to know that he was aware that the Princess had appointed a spy - someone to keep an eye on Kitty and report back to her every night at the zenana. If so, he had done it very cleverly without sounding disloyal to his wife or having to spell it out, in so many words.

Chapter Fourteen

By the time Rachel got back from her walk with Nanny Rosie, it was almost lunch time and Jeremy had returned from the hospital. He poked his head in to check if Rachel was back in her room. He found her sitting in one of the armchairs near the window, lost in thought. She got up to greet him and gave him a peck on the cheek before he sat in the other armchair. He put a large manila envelope on the marble topped table between them.

Jeremy told her that despite the primitive lab equipment, Dr. Saunders had been quite thorough in his autopsy. The results were indeed strange and baffling. The doctor was no criminologist but he had managed to take some photographs of the head which Jeremy had brought back with him. He warned Rachel that they were grisly but she wanted to see them. One picture in particular caught her attention.

'Jeremy, she looks like she has a bruise on her right temple. Colonel Riverton never mentioned that.'

'Let me see. Oh, that. Yes. Dr. Saunders says that was probably caused when her head hit the marble floor as she fell. She was found lying on her right side. It's there in the autopsy report.'

'I'll read that later. Let me tell you what I learnt from Nanny Rosie Dent,' she said, as she went on to brief him about little walk and talk with the nanny.

She had just finished bringing him up to date on her findings and conclusions when there was a discreet knock on the door. It was their Khidmatgar, Teji Singh who had come to remind them that lunch was about to be served.

As they walked downstairs, Jeremy said, 'Oh, I forgot to tell you. Colonel Riverton said he would like to show us Kitty's room after tea.'

'I'm sorry but we'll have to reschedule that. I already have a prior appointment after tea and I'll be busy at that time.'

'Busy doing what?'

'Taking flying lessons,' she answered cryptically, as they entered the dining hall and were greeted by the ADC – Sushanto Bose and the other staff members present.

Lunch was a subdued affair and Kitty gave up trying to make conversation after a few futile attempts at it. Rosie was not present as she took her meals in the nursery wing after feeding the children. Colonel Riverton was unusually quiet through the meal. Rachel realised that revisiting the crime with Jeremy and going over Kitty's autopsy report must have raked up unpleasant memories for him, all over again. And Elliot Wilkins, Sushanto Bose and Miss Martha remained polite but tight lipped. Rachel decided that she would get much further with them, if she met them individually. After lunch she informed Jeremy that she would spend the rest of the afternoon reading Kitty's journal.

II

Back in her room, she curled up on one of the arm chairs with Kitty's journal and began reading where she had left off;

I cannot believe that it has been only three days since we arrived at Dharanpore! We are out on a tiger shoot. It's all very exciting. Close to fifty royal guests including Teddy, Angela and myself left the Palace yesterday, mounted atop elephants. It was a grand procession of twenty elephants. We were made to sit on 'howdahs' – they are cushioned wooden boxes with wooden rails, saddled on to an elephant and can seat upto four people. The rails are so we don't topple over once the elephant starts walking, I suppose! I must admit it was scary at first. But once you get used to the gentle giant's gait and rhythmic movements, it gets quite comfortable. The mahout – which I learnt is the Hindi word for 'elephant handler', sits in front of the howdah on the elephant's neck and directs it to go at a certain pace in the chosen direction.

We've set up camp in a clearing in the jungle. It is early morning and though I slept fitfully in the tent, I was woken at dawn by a loud cacophony – only to remember that we were in the middle of a thick forest and the sound was the chirping of a thousand birds ...at any rate, that is what it sounded like to me. I had always thought that a jungle would be a deathly quiet place in the night, as I had read in a poem once - not a leaf moved, nor a twig cracked. That poet, quite obviously never spent a night in an Indian jungle! When the crickets stopped their mating racket, the frogs started, and then some jackals decided that one am was a perfectly good time to start a howling party! But I was so tired that all these sounds just became background noise and after a point, I just drifted off into a dreamless sleep.

The elephants surround the camp and I was told that most wild animals including wild elephants avoid getting into skirmishes with these gentle giants, like plague. Dickie says that a herd of elephants around a camp is the greatest safety blanket one can hope for, in a dense jungle like this.

The next entry read;

It has been an absolutely divine adventure so far. We lit a bonfire in the camp last night and had our dinner around it. I'm having the time of my life! Although my room-mate or should I say tent-mate, Angela has been grumbling non-stop about practically everything – starting with the mosquitoes that find ingenious ways to get inside our mosquito nets at night, to the open air makeshift sanitation facilities that offer very little privacy. She claims, that a party of wild pigeons, a few monkeys and two voyeuristic toads watched her intently as she had a bucket bath in our open air lavatory! I repeated her story to Dickie and he couldn't stop laughing! He finally spluttered – 'Now there's a sight those poor animals are not going to forget!'

The exciting part is that this morning, we got news of a kill about two miles away where a goat had been tethered to a tree. The beaters have surrounded that area and we will be setting off now on our elephants and hopefully we'll get a shot at the tiger!

Then came the entry with the sketch of a tiger that Rachel had seen earlier – the one that reminded her of King George; Kitty described how the cornered tiger had charged at their elephant. Luckily the elephant had stood its ground and Teddy had got a good shot.

When we returned to camp we heard that two other members of the hunting party had also been lucky. So far, we have three tiger skins.

The next entry read;

A.B has been in a black funk all evening. Our third day on the tiger shoot and the four of us – Dickie, A.B, Angela and I were atop the same elephant when we spotted a huge tiger. It was really beautiful and when it turned to look at us, even from a distance, one could see a white mark on its forehead. As I picked up my rifle and aimed, Dickie whispered softly, 'Don't shoot, Kitty. That tiger is protected by the shrine of the sacred river goddess. Well, I suppose you could try but I reckon you won't have much luck.'

I glanced to see if he was joking but when I saw he really meant it, I put my rifle down slowly. A.B, of course shushed him, took aim and fired. The gorgeous beast simply looked back at us with an alarmed expression and sprinted away unhurt.

A.B. was flummoxed! For the rest of the day, he kept muttering – 'I don't understand it! I had him!'

Dickie finally shut him up by saying, 'I told you, that tiger is protected by the sacred river goddess. It's not your fault you missed. As you can see, no one has succeeded in bagging him yet. And I wouldn't bet on it in the future either.' A.B just shook his head in disbelief. Personally, I don't know what to make of it – as Shakespeare made not too fine a point of it but... 'There are more things in heaven and earth, Horatio...' and leave it at that.

Chapter Fifteen

By the time Rachel finished reading the entries about the tiger shoot she realised it was tea time. She went downstairs to find the others and the Khidmatgar informed her that tea had been laid out for them, in the private garden. Sushanto Bose joined her in the foyer and offered to escort her.

'So, have you had any breakthroughs yet? In the case, that is,' he asked her casually, as they walked along a long corridor.

'Not yet, I'm afraid. Everyone seems to be so tightly wound up and there is a sort of 'cloud of secrecy' that hangs over anything to do with Kitty, as though, no one wants to really know what happened that night and they just want to brush her murder under a rug and forget it ever happened.'

'Can you blame us? A young woman murdered and the crown ruby stolen from under our very noses within the Palace grounds. We even conducted a thorough search through all the staff and guest rooms in the Palace and it yielded nothing. The guards were certain that no one had left the Palace grounds and yet the jewel had simply vanished into the night! It was a very unpleasant ordeal for all concerned.'

'But surely, most people would want to come forward and help with the investigation, if they saw or heard anything that night. So far, no one has come forward. Getting information from you all, feels like, oh, how can I put... it feels like I'm pulling teeth!'

'Well, I can't speak for the others but you can ask me anything you want about that night and I will tell you.'

'Alright, for starters, where were you between one and three am?'

'With the Prince. We were going through the agenda of his upcoming meeting at the Chamber of Princes to be held at the Taj Mahal Hotel in Bombay, where the Royals that represent the Salute States meet from time to time and discuss royal policy among other things.'

'Till three am?'

'Till four actually because this particular meeting was extremely important. It was to decide upon the stand the Royals would take jointly, if India were to regain her Independence from the British Raj. And what would be discussed and decided upon in this particular meeting, could have a crucial and lasting effect on the governance of independent Royal States and their very existence in independent India.'

'Why would the Royals need to take a stand?'

'Do you really want to know? I can tell you now, that it has no bearing whatsoever on the case you are investigating.'

'But it is interesting, nevertheless. Please do go on.'

'To begin with, the Royals knew exactly where they stood in British India. The British had always been perfectly clear that as long as they were aligned to the King-Emperor or Queen-Empress, they would not interfere with Royal Indian States. But, here comes the tricky part. That would not be the case if the British left. There was a great deal of ambiguity when it came to the Indian Congress Party. The royals knew that should the said Congress Party come into power, they would probably make a move to abolish monarchy altogether, post independence. And that would mean that the collective State taxes would no longer go into the exchequer of the ruler but to the Central government. There is also some talk currently amongst the top Congress Party members about abolishing Privy Purses in future and that would mean putting an end to Indian Royalty as we know it – one that has been around for thousands of years!'

'And now that you have Independence, has it come to pass?'

'Not yet but it could happen any day. The threat looms large over our heads like the proverbial sword of Damocles.'

'I see.'

'And I hope you can also see that the Prince and I were completely engrossed and occupied with State affairs, on the night in question, when Miss Riverton was killed.'

'And you saw and heard nothing?'

'Absolutely nothing. We were ensconced in the Prince's study for the better part of the night and I went to bed at about four thirty and was woken up an hour later with the news that Miss Riverton had been found murdered.'

'But you conducted the investigation that morning along with Colonel Riverton. What about the others? You must have narrowed down the list of suspects.'

'Well, yes. But everyone we questioned seemed to have a watertight alibi for the time of death!'

'That's interesting. What were their alibis?'

'Colonel Riverton said that he and Teddy were playing cards till three am with two other ICS men. Although I didn't really suspect either, I personally double checked with those chaps just to be sure. They confirmed his story.'

'What about Elliot Wilkins, Nanny Rosie and Miss Martha?'

'All three claimed that they were fast asleep at the time. We didn't have any reason to disbelieve any of them. Personally, I don't think any of them had anything to do with the murder and as far as Nanny Rosie and Miss Martha were concerned, their bedroom doors open out onto the nursery. And the amah who slept on the floor of the nursery that night, was quite sure that both their room doors stayed shut all night long. She did mention that she heard voices in the corridor at night but then she assumed that they belonged to the guests who had stayed on, after the banquet had ended.'

'That isn't as watertight as one could hope for since their rooms are on the ground floor and they could have easily come and gone through the French windows.'

'Yes but you are forgetting that there is always a sentry posted outside the Royal nursery. And he would have noticed any such movement and reported it.'

'And is there is no possibility that this sentry could have dozed off in the night?'

'Yes, there is that possibility but then these chaps are well trained. Even if he did doze off, he would've awoken at the slightest sound.'

'Right, what about the others?'

'Arthur Blackwell was embarrassed to admit it, but apparently, he spent the night with his fiancée - Angela and left her room only at about five in the morning.'

'Oh! I didn't know they were engaged at the time!'

'We didn't either. I can tell you it came as quite a shock to both Colonel Riverton and me when he confessed that he had been in Angela's room between one and five am. And he told me later that he would have liked to break the news of their sudden engagement to the Colonel, at a more peaceful time. But that his hand was forced, owing to the fact that this was a murder investigation and he had no other choice but to be honest about his whereabouts.'

'Did you even ask Angela, if it was true? Did she corroborate his story?'

'Of course! Lady Markham, we were conducting a murder investigation. We could hardly afford to cater to a lady's modesty or delicacy, under the circumstances. Good for her that she had the sense to be honest about it. If it hadn't been for this, I can tell you that Angela would have been a prime suspect as far as I was concerned. The way things were, any fool could see that there was no love lost between the two sisters.'

'I see. That just leaves the two royal couples.'

'Oh no, the younger Prince – Yuvraj Dharan and Princess Tara Devi were not in Dharanpore at the time of the murder. They had news that Princess Tara Devi's father had passed away and they had left two days before Miss Riverton's murder, to attend her father's funeral at Palanpur – the Princess' home town.'

'I didn't know that.'

'It's true. And Prince Dickie, as you know, was with me and Princess Uma Devi was in the zenana. And needless to say, the zenana is guarded by two sentries on rotation. Plus the Princess had a new born baby to nurture. I doubt if she had the time or the inclination to go about murdering people in the dead of the night. My wife just had a baby and I can tell you from personal experience, that she's so sleep deprived and exhausted by the baby's demands, around the clock that she uses any free time she gets, to catch up on her sleep,' he said with a smile.

'Oh, I didn't know that. Congratulations. Is it a girl or a boy?'

'I have been blessed with a daughter. My wife was rather keen on having a boy but I always wanted a little girl.'

'That is sweet. And are they here, at Dharanpore?'

'They just got back a week ago from Calcutta. All this while, they were at my wife's maternal home. In Bengal – the place I hail from, women go to their mother's house to give birth and then come back to their husband and in-laws only after a month or two. I suppose, it's only fair since it is a difficult time for any woman and the custom is designed to provide the maximum support and comfort to the young mother and the infant. Plus, I'm sure it is much nicer for the new mother to be in familiar surroundings, of the home she grew up in.'

'Absolutely. I couldn't agree more. What a thoughtful custom,' Rachel said with a smile.

II

They finally reached the garden, where tea tables had been laid out and the little Princess, Padma ran up to greet her, 'Rachel, you've come! Mummy said that I could have my tea here with you, instead of the nursery, as a treat!'

'How delightful! That was very nice of your mummy,' she said to the little girl, as she smiled at her mother.

Princess Uma spoke with a smile, 'My daughter is a very persuasive little girl and she seems to have taken quite a shine to you, Rachel.'

'I am glad to hear that. She is a lovely, well brought up child, Princess. What's more, she has also very kindly deigned to be my flight instructress.'

'Only if she finishes her glass of milk and sandwiches,' Princess Uma said with an indulgent smile at Padma, who started draining her glass of milk at once, as if on cue.

The bearer poured the tea from the silver service and handed Rachel a delicate bone china cup and saucer with the Dharanpore royal crest monogrammed on it, in gold.

Rachel took a sip and asked the Princess, 'I've been meaning to ask you, Princess. Whatever happened to the amah, who was attacked by Sheba?'

'Oh, she was alright. Other than the injury she sustained on her leg from the fall, she was fine. Luckily, Sheba didn't do her much harm but after that night I absolutely insisted that the leopard be kept in her cage, going forwards.'

'But His Highness gave me to understand that she was let loose two nights later – and was on the grounds when Kitty Riverton was killed.'

'Oh, no! He is mistaken. I remember those days he was very preoccupied with State Affairs. Sheba was most definitely caged. I remember because I was at the zenana – undergoing the traditional twenty-eight day seclusion with my baby at the time, and Sheba's cage is quite close to my wing at the zenana. I personally took steps to ensure the leopard would remain caged. My Khidmatgar – Bahadur Singh saw to it.'

'But there was an attack on Arthur Blackwell a few nights later.'

'Yes, I believe her cage door was left open by mistake after she was given her meal that night. You see Bahadur Singh had left for Bombay with the Prince and he had delegated the task of looking after Sheba to a new Khidmatgar.'

'Are you telling me that the Prince left for Bombay the very next day after Kitty Riverton was killed?'

'Well, yes. He couldn't possibly miss out on something as important, as the meeting of the Chamber of Princes, just because Miss Riverton died! I don't mean to sound heartless but life does go on and I pushed him to go. He knew it was for the best - it was a crucial meeting that would decide the future of Indian Royalty and...'

Rachel cut her short, 'Yes, so I've heard from Mr. Bose. Coming back to the attack on Arthur Blackwell...'

'Where was I? As I was saying, the new Khidmatgar, who was left in charge of Sheba, naturally denied that he had left the cage door open but then he was probably frightened of the consequences. Luckily for Mr. Blackwell, one of our guards intervened and Blackwell got away with a few superficial wounds and scratches. I shudder to think what may have happened, had the guard not heard his shouts.'

'I see. Your husband doesn't seem to think that Sheba is dangerous. But I wonder...'

'She is a full grown leopard, Rachel, with all the instincts of her species. I cannot concur with my husband on his blind spot, although I must admit that she is very well behaved around him and our children. But all the same, she is very unpredictable around others and I think the cage is the best place for her. It's within walking distance from here and they can visit her as often as they want to.'

'I agree with you. I'm also curious to see where her cage is. Can someone show me?'

'Of course! Teji Singh – please show Memsaab, Sheba's cage after tea.'

'No mummy – I'll show Rachel, please, may I?'

'Alright, darling. But be careful and no playing with Sheba. Teji Singh will go with you.'

Rachel spoke, 'Just one more thing, Princess. I would like to have a word with the amah, if she's still around.'

'I suppose that can be arranged but...,' she said, looking a little hassled, as if she was trying to find excuses to avoid Rachel from interrogating the amah, and continued, 'But I don't see what good can come of it, she'll just be alarmed and she doesn't speak a word of English.'

'Oh, that's alright. I'll be gentle with her. And I can get Colonel Riverton or Teji Singh to translate for me,' Rachel responded nonchalantly, as she thought to herself, *it's getting more and more like pulling teeth, it is!*

Chapter Sixteen

Rachel was lost in thought and responded in monosyllables to the little girl's chatter as they walked to Sheba's cage. It was just behind some trees at the far end of the marble folly. The cage was more like a large iron solarium with a large leafy tree growing within it. It also contained a small room at the back which was presumably where Sheba slept. It reminded her of the large enclosures for big cats at the London Zoo. There was someone else there too, sitting on a bench placed near the cage. As they approached and he turned, she saw that it was Elliot Wilkins. He looked paler than usual and stuttered as he greeted them.

'Ggg...good evening, Lady Mm...Markham, Pp.. princess Padma. I didn't know anyone was going to be here. I cc...come here sometimes for a little peace and qq...quiet. I'll go.'

'No, don't go. It's a good job I found you, Mr. Wilkins. I've been meaning to ask you if we can meet alone. Now, is as good a time as any, I suppose. I have some questions.'

Little Padma had gone up to the iron bars and was calling Sheba. The leopard who was sitting on a tree branch in the enclosure, got up, stretched luxuriously and gracefully loped down to greet Padma.

Elliot Wilkins seemed nervous, he looked about and said, 'This is really not a good time. I need to go and plan some school work, if you'll excuse me,' he said, standing up and making a move to leave.

'Mr. Wilkins, if this is not a good time, pray, tell me, when and where I can meet you,' Rachel snapped, unable to hide her irritation.

'I'll let you know, I cc..can't talk to you here,' he said, with a meaningful glance at Teji Singh and Padma. The little girl had put her scrawny hands through the bars and was stroking Sheba. Rachel was worried but then she realised that Teji Singh was alert and keeping a watchful eye on both the little girl and the leopard. The leopard, immune to their worries, was soaking up the attention and the affection and licking Padma's hand in return. It was an idyllic picture of a girl with her pet and for a moment Rachel conceded that the Prince may have been right about her being more like a domesticated cat.

Bringing her attention back to Wilkins, she said, 'I see. You don't want anyone else around when we speak.'

'Yes... ssh...the walls have ears here,' he said and leaned over to her and whispered conspiratorially, 'I will send you a note, later.' Before she could respond, he briskly walked away from her.

More like the trees have ears! Wonder what he's so scared about! Rachel thought to herself. Just then she heard the bushes behind her rustle, as though someone was moving through them. She whipped around and asked, 'Who's there?'

There was no response. Everything was quiet once more. She thought that Wilkins' nervousness had rubbed off on her and she would be better off, if she quelled her sense of uneasiness. She went forward to meet Sheba.

II

After dinner that night, Rachel asked Jeremy and Colonel Riverton out for a walk. She shared her fears with him that they were getting nowhere in the investigation and that time was running out. People around were being secretive and tight lipped and she felt disheartened and was at a loss, as to what to do next.

Colonel Riverton heard her out and said, 'In that case, I have some news that might cheer you up. I had a wire from my son-in-law, Arthur Blackwell, earlier today. They – that is Arthur, Angela and the twins, are stopping over in India on their way to Hong Kong, where he has accepted a new post as the head of a British trading company. He wired from the ship to inform me that they will be arriving here at Dharanpore in two days.'

'That is good news! But you must have known about this earlier. Why didn't you tell us?' Rachel asked plaintively.

'Thing is, I knew that they had planned a ten day stopover at Bombay but I wasn't sure if they would come all the way to Dharanpore with two small children. Angela had told me it sounded like a lot of hard work. Plus as you know, with communal riots flaring up all over the country, a long train journey is hardly safe or advisable at this time. So I didn't push them to come here either.'

Rachel said, 'I hadn't thought of that. I wonder what made them change their minds. Will it be safe for them to travel now?'

'Oh yes, as safe as it can get. You see, the Prince has very kindly offered them the use of his private airplane – to fly them here and back to Bombay.'

Jeremy said, 'That was a very thoughtful gesture on his part.'

'Yes, and I can tell you that the Prince wants to leave no stone unturned to get to the bottom of this case. Aside from the ease of their travel arrangements, it could also be that upon learning from me that you both were here, to reopen Kitty's murder case, Arthur probably managed to convince Angela that they were duty bound to help out in this investigation.'

'Well, I am grateful for whatever it is, that helped change their minds about coming here. We could certainly use their help. How long will they be staying here?' Rachel asked.

'Only for a week, I'm afraid. Their passage to Hong Kong is booked for the twentieth. Arthur has to report for his new duties by the first of next month. So they need to be in Hong Kong by the end of this month.'

Rachel smiled and said, 'A week is better than nothing, I suppose. Thank you, Colonel. I'm feeling better already.'

III

Later that night, Jeremy had gone to sleep in Rachel's room. Rachel herself was about to turn in when she heard a noise outside, in the corridor and then a rustling sound and saw that a piece of folded notepaper had been pushed under her door.

Rachel glanced at Jeremy. He was fast asleep. She padded up to the door in her bedroom slippers. Then in a quick move she opened her door and looked about. To her surprise, there was no one there. The corridor was dimly lit but she could still see clearly. Whoever it was, had left. Back in her room, she closed her door and turned the key. Then she picked up and unfolded the piece of paper to read the cryptic words on it;

At the stroke of midnight, be at the place where the pen is mightier than the sword. Tell no one. E.W.

'Oh, bother!' She thought to herself, 'The fool and his paranoia! Why can't he just meet us at a reasonable hour? Besides, I have no idea where the school room is and I don't suppose Jeremy does either. Stroke of midnight, indeed!'

Then she got under the covers and grumbled to herself, 'I'll deal with him in the morning,' as she turned out the lights.

Chapter Seventeen

The next morning Elliot Wilkins was not to be seen at the breakfast table. Rachel assumed that he had slept late after staying awake and keeping vigil for the midnight rendezvous that he had proposed. She didn't think anything more of it.

After breakfast, Colonel Riverton offered to show them Kitty's room and she readily agreed. Perhaps she would find some clues there as to her mysterious murder.

Rachel was surprised to see that Kitty's room was just a few doors away from theirs, on the same side. As the Colonel unlocked the door and they walked in, Rachel looked about. Kitty's room was very similar to hers, although being a single room; it was slightly smaller, had only two windows and no connecting door to the next room. She also noticed that because the colour scheme was lighter, and the soft furnishings were in peach and gold, the room looked brighter than hers. There was less furniture too. A single four poster bed was flanked by a two door wardrobe and a small settee. A study table and chair faced the windows. There was a door near the first window that led to her dressing room and the bath, which was shared by the next room.

Rachel asked, 'Colonel, who was in the room next to her, the one that shares the bath with this one?'

'Why, Angela, of course.'

'Right,' Rachel said, as she walked towards the closet and opened the double doors. Here, everything was as Kitty had left it. Rachel touched the silks, chiffons and taffetas of different lengths that were hanging on the left side. There were evening gowns, tea gowns, morning dresses and casual day frocks. There were several pairs of shoes, in the shoe rack below. She opened the drawers on the right to see that they were filled with the highest quality of lace, silk and satin lingerie. There were at least a dozen pairs of sheer silk stockings, some had not even been opened and were in their original Parisian packaging. She noticed that the clothes were not only of good cut and quality but some of the labels made her head swirl. Kitty had indeed spent a fortune on her new wardrobe.

There was a vanity case filled with a variety of trinkets, bracelets, bead necklaces, brooches and pearl pins. Hatboxes were on the top shelf. If these had all been newly bought, just after the war, which Rachel believed to be true, judging from the styles, she realised that Kitty had not been jesting when wrote in her journal that they had cost the earth. They would have. Rationing had become worse after the war and things like fine silk stockings and lace lingerie could only be found on the black market, that too at double, sometimes triple the original prices! And that went for most of the haute couture labels displayed on the dresses. To her mind this seemed extraordinary. Where would a WAAF recruit get the money to buy fine clothing like this?

She turned towards Colonel Riverton who was with Jeremy at the study table. They were going through papers, travel documents and odds and ends and asked, 'Colonel, this may sound like a strange question but exactly how rich was your daughter?'

'Eh, what? Whatever do you mean?'

'Was she wealthy? Had she come into a legacy?'

'Well, yes a smallish one from her maternal aunt, my wife's sister who died in the war and left her a cottage in the country and a small annuity, but why do you ask?'

'Because this is just a rough estimate, I mean, it could be a lot more, but Kitty seems to have spent about two thousand pounds on a new wardrobe for herself before she came out to India.'

The Colonel was shell shocked. He spluttered, 'Two thousand pounds! On clothes! Why, that's impossible! She couldn't have been stupid enough to sell the cottage to buy bloody clothes. Anyhow, I don't think a house in the country would have fetched that much after the war. Maybe less than half that amount. You must be mistaken.'

'There is no mistake, Colonel. These clothes would make a duchess proud.' Rachel went on to explain to Jeremy and the Colonel how she came to that figure, based on the labels and the quality of the things she had found.

The Colonel was still in a state of disbelief. He was shaking his head and muttering, 'Two thousand pounds on bloody clothes! Women are incalculable!'

'Did she have any other source of income?'

'Not to my knowledge, she didn't!'

'Then I wonder where she got the money from. Jeremy could you be an angel and wire Inspector Parker later. Ask him to get us details, you know, find out more about this legacy from her aunt. Perhaps he could also find out if she sold the cottage left to her.'

'Two thousand bally pounds on clothes!' The Colonel repeated.

'Relax, Colonel, look at it this way – if she hadn't been murdered, those two thousand pounds would have been well spent, don't you think? After all, they landed her a Prince!' Rachel said with a bright smile.

'That has got to be the stupidest thing I've ever heard. And I've heard enough. I have a headache. I think I had better go and lie down.'

'Alright, Colonel! I'll take some more time here. Do you mind if we give you back the key, later?'

'Yes, no. Keep the bally key. I can tell you this much, had I known, and if she hadn't been murdered, I would have shot her myself .Two thousand pounds on clothes, hmph! ' He muttered, as he left the room.

Rachel smiled and walked over to the desk where Jeremy was. 'So what do you make of it?'

'Are you quite sure, darling? I mean couldn't these be cheap imitations or what they call 'rip offs' of the originals?'

'Darling, how many times do I have to tell you that when it comes to clothes and shoes, never ever question my judgement. Years and years of training have gone into it. I can spot an imitation, even a good one, from a mile!'

'Whatever you say, dear. Anyway come and take a look at this fountain pen! It's a Mont Blanc. Looks like her spending spree went beyond shoes and clothes.'

'Hmm, this silver pencil looks pretty unusual too,' she said, picking it up from the pen stand to examine its metal casing. 'It feels too heavy to write with though.'

'Why, what does it contain? Lead? Heh, heh,' Jeremy said chuckling at his own wit, as Rachel rolled her eyes.

'Darling, would you shoot me if I spent two thousand pounds on clothes?' Rachel asked with mock concern.

'No, my dear, I would probably have a coronary and that would only leave you with more money to spend.'

'Hmm. Interesting. Right, we ought to get back to work. What have you found so far?'

'Nothing much. Her papers seem to be in perfect order. From what I can see, she had a knack for being well organised. There's nothing here that explains a windfall though. If she was a cat burglar in disguise, she's covered her tracks rather well. I think we ought to pay more attention to her journal.'

Rachel agreed. 'Yes, I'll take out some time to read it completely tomorrow. I think we are done here. For now,

I want to find that Elliot chap and corner him into a hole until he tells me all I need to know!'

'I feel sorry for him already!' Jeremy said with a grin, as they walked out of Kitty's room and he locked the door.

Walking down the corridor, Rachel realised that she was still holding Kitty's heavy silver pencil in her hand. She had absentmindedly forgotten to put it back in the pen stand. She casually slipped it in to her skirt pocket making a mental note to go back and replace it later.

Chapter Eighteen

After lunch, Jeremy had gone to the Dharanpore post office to wire Inspector Parker regarding Kitty's legacy. Rachel decided she would go to the school room and check on Elliot Wilkins. The fact that he had been missing from the luncheon table as well had her worried. She asked Teji Singh to escort her to the school room. It was on the ground floor, across the courtyard from the nursery. She was puzzled to find it empty. Elliot Wilkins seemed to have disappeared. She then went to the nursery where she found Miss Martha seated at the table, reading a book. The children seemed to be missing too.

She greeted her. 'Good afternoon, Miss Martha. I was looking for Mr. Wilkins. He doesn't seem to be in the school room.'

'Shh,' she said with a finger on her lips. 'The children are taking their afternoon naps in the next room, Lady

Markham. And no, today is a Sunday so there is no school room,' she whispered.

Rachel whispered back, 'Of course, how silly of me! I seem to have lost track of days over here. It's just that Mr. Wilkins was missing from the breakfast table and now he seems to have skipped lunch as well. I just wanted to make sure he was alright.'

'That is very kind of you and I can assure you, he is fine. We did not skip breakfast. On Sundays, we usually take our breakfast early to ensure that we attend Sunday mass on time. He accompanied me to the Church this morning. And he was not present for luncheon because he teaches Sunday school at the Dharanpore Missionary School for Boys, so he will be back only by four.'

'I see. Thank you,' she whispered as she turned around to leave.

'Lady Markham, if you have time, I wish to have a word with you.'

'Yes?'

'Perhaps we can talk in the courtyard where we can speak more freely,' she said softly, as she put her book down. Rachel realised that she had been reading the Bible.

'What about the children?' Rachel whispered nodding in their direction.

Miss Martha whispered back with a smile, 'The amah is in the room with them. They will be fine. Come with me.'

Rachel followed her out meekly. She had a strange sensation of being transported back to her own school days.

The courtyard had a central fountain with a few ornately carved wooden benches placed around it. Miss Martha chose one that was in the shade and beckoned Rachel to sit next to her. The sound of cascading water had a soothing effect and created a cool and peaceful atmosphere around them.

As Rachel sat down, Miss Martha looked at her and said in a hushed voice, 'I'll come straight to the point. I am aware that you and your husband are here to investigate that woman's death.'

'Yes, we are, although strangely that seems to be the worst kept secret in this Palace,' Rachel whispered back with a smile, wondering why they were still whispering.

As if on cue, Miss Martha said in a normal voice, 'We can speak freely here. I meant to speak with you earlier but I suppose you have been busy trying to solve this crime.'

'That is right.'

'May I be frank? It is about that woman I wish to speak.'

'Miss Kitty Riverton?'

'Yes. Whatever little interaction I had with her, I came to the conclusion that she brought misfortune upon herself.'

'What makes you say that?' Rachel asked.

'Why, her behaviour, of course! It was atrocious, the way she went on, like a common little hussy chasing after the Prince like that. A real lady would never do that - leading a married man to lust and sin.'

Rachel smiled inwardly and thought, *I wonder what Miss Martha would say if I told her what real ladies did in the social whirl of London society.* Rachel could name half a dozen titled ladies who she knew, were busy having affairs with married men.

Outwardly she kept a straight face and said, 'Indeed? That does seem shocking. But surely, the married man in the equation, ought to share some of the blame, in an affair of this sort?'

'A man can't be blamed, they have... urges. It is up to women to withhold the sanctity of life and relationships.'

Rachel groaned inwardly but said nothing to contradict Miss Martha's medieval views on men and women.

Miss Martha continued, 'Besides, the Prince didn't stand a chance. It was quite evident to me, right from the start – the very first evening at that royal banquet that she was out to get him and in the end, she did.'

'I heard a rumour that they were engaged to be married. Could there be any truth it?'

'I suppose there could be. I never heard a formal announcement but then how else could one explain her walking about brazenly, wearing all that royal jewellery that rightfully belonged to his wife?'

'But I've been given to believe that it is normal for an Indian Prince to take on multiple wives. So could it be possible that Kitty was gifted the jewellery by her fiancé and wouldn't that make it alright?'

'Certainly not! She was a Christian woman and as such had no business to be chasing His Highness in the first place. There were so many nice English boys about, that night. The right thing to do would have been to marry one of them. A lady would have done so. But I can tell you that she was neither a lady nor a good Christian. And she deserved everything she got.'

'I can see your point of view but surely getting brutally murdered is far too harsh a punishment for any young girl, whatever her actions may have been.'

'The fires of Hell are her punishment for tempting a heathen,' she said with conviction and her eyes shone with the gleam of a fanatic who could visualize the hell fire.

Rachel was tempted to ask Miss Martha if her visions of hell fire did not extend to those who were 'employed' by a heathen. But then she was wary and she knew from experience that there would be nothing to gain by creating an enemy.

Rachel spoke up. 'Incidentally, can you recall your movements on the night that Miss Riverton was killed? I was just wondering if you saw or heard anything unusual.'

'Let me see. I remember her coming in to the nursery dressed up like Jezebel to say goodnight to Padma after dinner. Then when little Padma asked if she could read her a bed time story, she made up some excuse about having to go and to meet her sister. She kissed her goodnight. The wretched woman even had the audacity to give me a flying kiss as she went out.'

Rachel struggled to keep a straight face as she pictured the scene. 'I see, and afterwards?'

'I got up for a glass of water and looked out the French windows and I did see her strolling about with her sister on the grounds. They seemed to be having a heated conversation almost as if they were arguing over something.'

'What time was this?'

'It was quite late. I remember hearing the nursery clock sound its half hourly chime and noticed that it was half past twelve.'

'I see. Did you see or hear anything after that?' Rachel asked, wondering if Miss Martha had anything to do with precipitating Kitty's journey towards the hell fire, she had so fervently wished upon her. She certainly hated her enough.

'I couldn't get back to sleep and about an hour later, I thought I heard a door bang somewhere close by. I remember thinking how inconsiderate it was, considering people in the Palace were trying to get some sleep. It was all quiet after that and then just as I was going back to sleep, I heard a man's voice outside in the corridor. And then a woman's voice.'

'Did you recognise the voices?'

'Not the woman's voice but I did recognise the man's and I remember wondering why Mr. Wilkins was up so late and who he was speaking to. After that, I'm afraid sleep took over and the next thing I know it was morning and there was complete pandemonium in the Palace because Miss Riverton had been killed.'

'Did you ask him the next day, what he was doing out in the corridor so late at night?'

'As a matter of fact, I did but he told me I must have mistaken someone else's voice for his. When I insisted that I had heard him, he informed me that I must have dreamt it because he had been in his room the entire night and had not ventured out.'

'Did you believe him?'

'I may be old but I am no fool. It was Mr. Wilkins alright. You see, he has a peculiarity in his speech. He tends to stammer when he is nervous.'

'Yes, I noticed that. Miss Martha, you have been extremely helpful. I can't thank you enough.'

'It is nothing, dear. I do hope you achieve your aims but mark my words, whoever did her in, did us all a favour! She was an adventuress and a fortune huntress and I am glad that she came to such a fitting end. This ought to serve as an example for other young women, who go about simply asking for trouble,' Miss Martha said, as she heaved herself up from the bench.

As far as Rachel was concerned, she was glad that their conversation had finally come to an end. Her patience was wearing thin and she did know how much more she could stand, being at the receiving end of Miss Martha's Victorian ideals for women.

Chapter Nineteen

Rachel glanced at her watch and realised it was only two in the afternoon. She had plenty of time before Elliot Wilkins got back from teaching Sunday school and decided to catch up on reading Kitty's journal.

She made herself comfortable on the arm chair in the room and began reading. The entries did not have dates on them but Rachel realised the next one must have been written a day or two after the hunting party had returned from the Tiger Shoot. She glanced over the page and read about the royal picnic that Nanny Rosie had spoken about. It was followed in the next few pages by a host of other royal events – polo matches, dinners and dances.

Throughout the diary and its flow, there was an underlying theme of an unbroken happiness as Kitty wrote about what Dickie had told her, what she had said to him, the things they had done together and so on. She flipped a few more pages until she came to an entry where Kitty's handwriting was visibly different from the breezy entries on the rest of the pages. The writing was so shaky and brittle that Rachel instinctively felt there was something amiss about it. She read on.

Today was such an awful day... made me realise how stupid I've been in giving away my heart so carelessly. There was a traditional Indian ceremony held in the honour of the new born Prince and his mother. We were all invited to attend. There he was, sitting around the sacred fire in a Hindu ritual with his wife and child, with a rather pleased expression upon his face. Little Padma was also at her mother's side. There was a great deal of chanting by a group of Brahmins and the head priest stopped from time to time to direct the couple to make their offerings into the sacred fire.

Everytime he had to tie something around his wife's neck or link his hand with hers as they put offerings into the fire together, I felt as though someone was walking all over my gut with hobnailed boots. I made myself sit through it for two long hours – possibly the longest two hours of my life! And left with the others only after seeing him close the ceremony by putting an enormous emerald necklace around her neck – a token of his love and regard, in return for the priceless gift that she had borne him - an heir to the throne.

I feel sick to my stomach although I don't know why I should feel this way, when I've known all along that he was a married man with children. I've even taken his daughter out on picnics and yet in my own way, I've conveniently ignored the existence of the Princess

– his lawful wedded wife and the mother of his two children. I suppose his wife was always a dim figure in the background and didn't seem quite real to me up until today. Today for the first time I saw her in the flesh and although she has just given birth to their child, she is very beautiful and looks at him with a certain look of proprietorship and love, one that I know well. I catch myself looking at him the same way when he is around. But she has the right to look and feel that way about him and I have been so very wrong...to the point of imbecility. Daddy was right all along. I must give him up. I have to! I can't see any other way out. Oh Dickie, my love! What will I do without you! I thought we had found the perfect love... oh God! Please help me...

Thereafter most of the words were blotted out as Rachel realised that the ink was washed away by what seemed to be the most likely explanation - Kitty's tears... *my heart is broken... wretchedness... desolation.... wish I... dead....painful... Arthur... survive this...*

She turned the page to read the next entry, written a day later.

A.B. is over the moon. I accepted his proposal of marriage earlier today. But more than A.B, Daddy seems to be thoroughly relieved. He's been smiling like a Cheshire cat ever since we broke the news to him! My father seems to be under some misguided notion that his tales of caution worked! Anyhow, he seems quite relieved and thinks I am over Dickie and that I have heeded his warnings. Little does he realise that no matter what happens Dickie is the only man I will ever love. No one can ever take that away from me. I love him to the point of madness but I suppose a love like that can never really be a happy thing. A.B tried to kiss me and it was positively revolting. I pushed him away and he thinks I'm being coy. If he only knew about the nights of passion I've dreamt about with Dickie!

Daddy got so carried away that he went and announced the news of our engagement. I have been smiling and accepting congratulations from almost everyone around the Palace today and yet I have never felt such deep despair in my life ever before. God help me!

The only person who didn't congratulate or wish us was Dickie. At dinner tonight he kept looking at me intensely and I think he was the only one who could see through my false smile and glimpse my despair. He never once took his eyes off me, not even for a moment. Luckily A.B didn't notice but then he never really does. He is too busy being important and talking about the ICS most of the time. What a bore! But Dickie and I must behave ourselves for A.B's sake, now that I am to be his wife. I must speak to Dickie about the way he still looks at me. It won't do to cause a scandal, even if we are in love. I don't want our passion for one another ruining our lives with our respective spouses. Must go now – there's a knock at the door. Probably Angela – yet another person who can bore me to tears without having to even open her mouth. In a perfect world A.B and Angela ought to be married – they seem to be made for each other.

At this point in the narrative, Rachel stopped to think how prophetic Kitty had been, albeit unknowingly about Arthur Blackwell and Angela's union. Life was strange indeed. She was compelled to read on. Her eyes opened wide in surprise as she read the first line of the next page.

I was a girl up until yesterday and I awoke in a woman's body today.

I cannot recognise this happy, glowing, beautiful woman I see in the mirror. He just left a few minutes ago but I can't seem to stop smiling or blushing for that matter. I share the incandescent dizziness of a bride in love. A bride who has been thoroughly loved, mind, body and soul – can it really be me? What can I write that would do justice to what happened last night. Oh bliss!

I opened the door last night only to find Dickie standing there. He came in and closed the door behind him as I rushed to cover my flimsy night gown with the wrap. He said nothing as he walked towards me and spun me around to face him. There was no gentleness in his touch. He looked into my eyes, his own blazing with a fire and fury I had never seen before. Strangely I felt no fear as he told me with barely controlled anger, 'You are mine, Kitty. You can never belong to another man.' Then his mouth covered mine passionately. You could have knocked me down with a feather. My knees buckled and he carried me to the bed. After that I lost track of my senses completely...

At some point after dawn as the early morning Sun shone into the room and we awoke sleepily in each other's arms, he took me once again. In the midst of our throes of passion, I vaguely remember that I heard my dressing room door open and a small shriek as Angela saw us and then bolted, she must've had the shock of her life.

Silly of us not to have locked the door but there it is. Stuffy old Angela can do what she likes. I am beyond all earthly cares as I tread at heaven's door. From here on, I am answerable only to him. I belong to him and him only, mind, body and soul and all else can fade away into oblivion, for all I care!

Rachel wondered if the Prince knew about the existence of this diary. Moreover, she wondered if the Colonel had bothered reading up to this part. She thought not. He probably hadn't had the patience. As per his own admission he had claimed that he didn't know what *'went on between those two'* but this particular entry left no room for ambiguity in Rachel's mind as to what had really taken place and had clearly marked the point-of-no-return thereafter, 'for those two'.

Chapter Twenty

Rachel looked about to find a safe hiding place for the journal. She finally hid it under her mattress. Up until now she had not realised just how important it was to their investigation. This was precious inside information straight from the horse's mouth and without it she would be far more clueless than she currently was. Amidst all the secrecy and darkness that surrounded Kitty's death, the light was slowly becoming clearer, almost as if Kitty herself was guiding her towards the truth. At least now she had far more clarity regarding the dynamics between her and the rest of the people in this drama – The Prince, Angela, Arthur Blackwell and Colonel Riverton. And she hoped that there would be more. She realised that she was clutching at straws but she wanted to know if Kitty had written more about Princess Uma's reaction or Arthur Blackwell's shock at Kitty's new found status as the Prince's mistress or fiancé. Or about anyone else in the Palace who had reason enough to hate her with a vengeance. She promised herself that she would read the rest of it later that night even if it meant staying up all night.

It was five thirty in the evening and Rachel decided it was time to hunt down Elliot Wilkins and confront him with what she had learned from Miss Martha, about the fateful night.

She sent Teji Singh with a note to Elliot's room. Teji came back with the note ten minutes later, only to inform her that he was not in his room. Rachel decided she would go in search for him, on her own. After visiting all his usual haunts – the school room, writing room and library, and not finding him there, Rachel thought she would take a chance and see if he was sitting on the bench near Sheba's cage. He was.

'I've been looking for you, Mr. Wilkins. I'm sorry I couldn't keep our appointment last night.'

'I...I was just wondering why you didn't show up.'

'Well, you hadn't taken into account that we are new here and that neither Jeremy nor I had any idea where the school room was and your note specifically requested that we tell no one. I couldn't see how we could accomplish both objectives without asking someone for directions in the middle of the night!'

'I...'m so sorry I didn't realise I was putting you in a conundrum. You were right of course, in nn...not coming.'

'Well, never mind right or wrong, here I am now, and as you can see, quite alone. Do you think we can speak freely here? There doesn't seem to be anyone else around, well except for Sheba of course. Hello, Sheba, old girl, 'Rachel said waving at the leopard, who yawned back at her in greeting from her perch on the tree.

'Bb...but we can still be seen by anyone who passes by.'

'Is there a problem with that?'

'Yes. There are ww..wheels within wheels. You don't ss...seem to realise what you've gotten yourself into. There is dd...danger, great danger if anyone sees us.'

'So what do you propose? We do need to talk at some point, you know.'

'Come with me. Dd..do You know where the library is?'

Rachel nodded.

'Right. There is a passage right after you cross it. At the end of the passage, you will find a green door. If you go through that door you will find a small winding staircase going up that takes you directly up to the Palace roof. It is hardly used by anyone but the servants, and th...that too on rare occasions when the roof has to be lit up or decorated. I will go up there and wait for you and you can join me after ten minutes. Just make sure that no one notices you entering the passage or the stairwell. It is of vital importance. There are ww...wheels...'

'Yes, yes, within wheels. You mentioned that a few moments ago. Well, go on and I'll follow and yes, I will be careful that no one is about, when I do.'

Fifteen minutes later Rachel found herself high up on the Palace ramparts. The view was breathtaking and she could see for miles on all sides. The evening Sun was mellow and there was a pleasant breeze that played with her hair as she walked towards Elliot.

Rachel said, 'Why, it's lovely up here! Such a pity that the family doesn't use this space.'

'It's supposed to be haunted by a Maharani who committed suicide by jumping off these ramparts two hundred years ago and has been considered unlucky ever since.'

'Really. How interesting. Have you seen her ghost?'

'Can't say I have, though the servants refuse to come up here after dark and that makes it my favourite sanctum sanctorum when I want to get away from all that goes on downstairs.'

'Yes. I suppose this Palace – with all its people and the lack of privacy, can get to you after a point. However, I am sure you didn't invite me up here to speak about ghouls or Palace politics. So let's get down to the business at hand.'

'Cccc..certainly, what would you like to know?'

'Well, there is the question of what you were doing, roaming about the Palace and perhaps the grounds, on the night that Kitty was killed,' Rachel said coming straight to the point.

'Nn...no... I was...'

'Don't bother denying it Elliot. I already know that you were out there and probably saw something that night, which in turn, scared the living daylights out of you. But what I don't know is, what you saw – or rather who you saw and why you've kept quiet about it for so long!'

'Well, it's all very well for you – you get to waltz in and ask your questions and then whether or not you find out what happened, you will leave. I, on the other hand, have to live here and go on living here for God knows how long.'

'Why? I mean, why do you have to go on living here if you despise it so much? Surely, you have that option as well. You're a free man... oh, I see. There is something in your past that won't allow it. Look here, Elliot, whatever it is, I don't want to know and I don't want to pry unless it has anything to do with Kitty's death.'

'It has nothing to do with any of this, Ll..lady Markham...' he responded indignantly.

'Call me Rachel, please!'

'Alright Rachel, if you must know, I was thrown out of Harrow because they caught me stealing school supplies more than once. It wasn't much and since I returned whatever I had taken, it was all settled very quietly. But I hhh...have a problem... sometimes I don't know what comes over me and I pick up things that don't belong to me. Anyhow, because of this malady I suffer from, I will never get a teaching job in England again. The powers that be at Harrow made quite sure of that. I was jobless for over a year and at the point of starvation when Colonel Riverton showed me great kindness by recommending me for this position here. And I can't ask for more – my duties are light, all my needs are taken care of and I lack nothing here. I will always be grateful to him.'

'And yet you show your gratitude by shielding the person who murdered his daughter in cold blood!'

'Can't you see I have been dealt with no other choice?'

'Well, I can see that someone here has caught on to your past and has probably been blackmailing you. Possibly threatening to disclose your secret to your employers so you lose your position here. Who is it Elliot?'

'It isn't like that. Colonel Riverton hadn't duped the royal family in hiring me – on the contrary, he had been honest with them. It was just that he gave them a slightly watered down version about my background. But there was blackmail - of a different sort. I don't know if I can explain it.'

'Well, you had better try. Or I will be left with no choice but to draw my own conclusions that you are playing a very clever little game to shield yourself from a dastardly crime against your benefactor's daughter.'

'No!' He shouted. 'I admired Kitty more than all those men put together, men who preyed upon her innocence like a pack of wolves. Don't think I don't know what went on within these walls. She was a fine girl and I would've done anything to protect her but it was all over before I could do anything. The only thing left was Hobson's choice. Nothing could bring her back from the dead and trying to get her justice would only achieve one end – losing my job and going back to live on starvation street once again.'

'So you chose to save your own hide? Very commendable for someone who claims to have been her greatest admirer, I must say,' Rachel said, unable to control the sarcastic sting that flew from her lips.

'How can I make you understand? It was not so much about saving my own hide, as you put it but more to the question of who would believe me if I spoke the truth. It was a toss-up between a poor tutor's word against someone who couldn't be touched.'

'Try me.' Rachel said, as he shook his head sadly. She continued, 'Or just tell me who it was, you spoke to, in the corridor that night. Please, I'll do everything to keep your name from coming up in this investigation. You will have nothing to worry about. I give you my word on that. Just please, for once, be the man you would have liked to be for Kitty's sake.'

She could see the conflict raging within him before he answered, in a hushed voice, 'It was Her Highness – Princess Uma Devi. Now, will you believe me when I tell you that you have no idea what you're up against?'

Rachel answered simply, 'Yes, I believe you.'

They stood side by side facing the setting Sun, each lost in their own thoughts. The world around them seemed to have gone quiet.

Finally Rachel broke the silence. 'Tell me what happened that night.'

Chapter Twenty One

Elliot Wilkins spoke. 'I had gone to bed early, at about nine thirty but was later woken by a sudden noise in the middle of the night – like a door banging somewhere. Anyhow I tried to get back to sleep but I couldn't so I went for a little walk. I walked until I reached Sheba's cage and sat on that bench for a while. It was a quiet night. I remember there was a full moon. Then all of a sudden I heard a guttural sound like a gurgling cry that came directly from behind the bench I was sitting on. I can tell you, it nearly made me jump out of my skin! I got up to see what had made the sound and I saw an amah stepping out of the marble folly and realised that the sound must have come from a little further away, to be precise, from the marble folly. She couldn't see me as I was standing behind the bushes but I could see her clearly.

She had something in her hand that glinted in the moonlight. I saw that she was trying to wipe it. Then she looked about her furtively and tucked whatever it was, in the recesses of her sari. I started following her stealthily. Imagine my surprise when I found that she was heading directly towards the zenana, more specifically towards Princess Uma's wing in the zenana. She said something to the guard at the door. He went in to relay her message and after a while I saw that the Princess herself had come out. She and the amah walked a little distance away from the guard probably to get out of his earshot and I saw the amah talking in undertones, as if she was narrating something to the Princess. She then took out the thing she had hidden in her sari and gave it to the Princess. I didn't have my glasses on so I couldn't see very clearly but it looked as though, whatever the thing was, fitted in her palm. The Princess took it and tucked it away in her er... blouse. They spoke for some more time and then the amah left and started walking in my direction.

All this while I had been standing behind a pillar and I was in a precarious position. If I didn't move the amah would surely see me, as she would have to walk past me and if I did move, the Princess who was looking in our direction would be sure to notice me. I took my chances and moved slightly to my left but as I had suspected, the Princess spotted me and came towards me.

In my nervousness, I muttered something about having left my glasses in the school room but she was no fool. The school room was in the opposite direction across the courtyard and judging from my nervous state, she must've realised that I had seen or heard something that I was not supposed to. She asked me to walk down the corridor with her and then she told me in no uncertain terms that I was to keep quiet about whatever it is, I thought I had seen and heard or she would make sure that I would be incarcerated in Dharanpore prison for the rest of my life, on charges of theft and Kitty Riverton's murder! I was shell shocked to hear it. You see, I had no idea up until such time that Kitty had been murdered.

She also said that given my chequered past, it would be easy for her to convince her husband and everybody else that the amah had seen me murder Miss Riverton in order to rob her. I had no clue what she was talking about until I was informed the next morning that the priceless ruby necklace – the Pride of Dharanpore had been stolen as well. If I were asked, I was to say that I hadn't left my room all night and that I had slept well and in consequence, had seen and heard nothing. The Princess told me that if I did as she said, she would see to it that I would come to no harm and that I would be well taken care of for the rest of my life.

As it is, I was frightened out of my wits and I found myself stuttering and stammering and agreeing to everything she asked of me. I am ashamed to say but that is exactly what I did in the morning when I was given the sad news which confirmed Kitty's death. When Colonel Riverton questioned me, later that morning, I pretended that I hadn't seen or heard anything the previous night and no one had any reason to think that I had lied about it.

It's been two years since it all happened and not a single day goes by when I don't think of what I've done and I pray for Kitty's forgiveness and mercy. I pray that her soul finds peace. I haven't missed a single Sunday mass and try to make up for it by giving service to others but through it all, I carry the burden of guilt and the knowledge of my cowardice. And the fact that wherever she is, she probably *knows* that I've let her down. And that is the real story, Lady Markham and you can take it or leave it.'

Rachel said nothing for a while as she let it all sink in. Then she looked at him and said with kindness, 'Well, you've done the right thing by telling me the truth today and you need no longer carry such a heavy burden alone. I promise that Jeremy and I will do our best to see that Kitty gets the justice she deserves and I don't care, how many royal heads have to roll in order for it to happen.'

'Oh, that's easier said than done. This isn't England, you know. I don't see how you can get justice when the ten man police force here, takes orders directly from the royal family, not to mention that the royals are a law onto themselves, here at Dharanpore, as in all independent Royal States in India. And now that India has just got her independence you can't even appeal to the Viceroy through a political officer anymore.'

'We'll have to find a way. India has her own judicial system now and perhaps we could appeal to someone high up in the British Foreign Office and the central government for help, if we can prove beyond a doubt that the Princess was responsible for Kitty's murder.'

'I doubt that either would have jurisdiction in an independent Royal State like Dharanpore unless of course at some point in the future, it merges into unified India. There is some talk about that being inevitable in a couple of years from now.'

'Then we'll just have to have patience and let the case come to trial when it does. But you can't let something like that get in the way of searching for the truth. First of all, we need to be sure that it was the amah, who killed Kitty on Princess Uma Devi's instruction. It would help if you could describe the murder weapon, if that is what it was – the thing that you saw the amah hand over to the Princess.'

'I can't. I couldn't see very well without my glasses but I did see it glint in the moonlight so I know for sure that it was something metallic.'

'That fits in with Dr. Saunders' autopsy report. Could it have been a collapsible dagger of some sort? Do they have any weapon like that in the Palace?'

'Not to my knowledge but then who knows what devilish weapons they may have.'

'Right. By the way, did this particular amah walk with a limp?'

'Yes, by Jove, I think she did. But how would you know something like that?'

'I have an idea about how we can build up the case against her without getting you directly involved.'

'How?'

'Leave it to me. I must go now and get cracking on this idea. Meanwhile act normally and don't worry. If you remember anything else from that night that you feel will help us along, just shove a note under my door like you did last night and we'll meet up here.'

Chapter
Twenty Two

Rachel couldn't wait to share what she had learnt, with Jeremy. He would know what to do. As she went downstairs, she encountered Teji Singh and asked him if he knew where Jeremy was. He informed her that he had gone somewhere with the Prince along with Colonel Riverton. Since Rachel had no idea when he would be back she decided to use the time before the dinner gong sounded, to read more of Kitty's journal.

Taking it out of the hiding place, she started reading.

It has been three days since Angela last spoke with me but as far as I'm concerned that is a blessing in disguise. However, she loses no opportunity to give me a disdainful glance, if our eyes meet over the dinner table, as if I were something that just crawled out from under a rock. It is funny she never joined a convent. Her outlook is so much like a nun's! Anyway, I know that this is the calm before the storm and that once she opens her mouth to give me a sermon on men and morals, I probably won't be able to shut her up for the next three days. Lord, I'd do anything to avoid that!

I have a new dour faced amah who has replaced my erstwhile cheerful one. Like Angela, she too has this look of disdain whenever I ask her to do something for me. She has these heavily kohl lined eyes and looks rather like an evil raccoon. I miss my old amah. At least, she used to smile a lot. I don't think this woman knows how to smile. When I asked her where my old amah had gone, she just shook her head and said something in Hindi, which of course went straight over my head. That reminds me, Dickie told me that I ought to learn the local language if I want to feel at home here at the Palace. He says he's going to speak to Elliot about getting me a Hindi tutor from the Dharanpore Missionary School for Boys. I agree with him, I might as well learn the local dialect if I have to live here for the rest of my life. The sooner, the better. I think I'll go and have a word with Elliot in a while and see how he's faring with the task. He is a queer little man. I think he's quite sweet in a strange way - the way he stammers whenever he speaks to me and follows me about with his sheep eyes.

Oh, yes, sheep eyes reminds me, the worst thing was that I had gone riding yesterday morning with the usual crowd and A.B was there too and he kept cantering up to me and trying to make conversation. It's the only time he could since I have been avoiding him like the plague for the past few days. I felt that it was high time that I informed him that we were no longer engaged. Poor chap, it's not his fault that I'm in love with someone else! But he was rather awful about it when I broke off our engagement after the ride. I thought he'd take it on the chin like a gentleman and not turn a hair. After all, it's not like we were ever in love. But what can I say, people are inscrutable.

He raved and ranted that I'd made him look like a fool... (Ha! As if I'd interfere with nature, it wasn't my fault if he was born to be one!) But I didn't say that to him of course. I wish I had though because moments later he informed me that 'everyone' including Angela had warned him against proposing to me and yet he had felt sorry for me and done so just to give me a chance at a decent life. He said he had no doubt that I'd end up as the Prince's mistress and spend the rest of my life in a sordid Indian harem and it would serve me right because the Prince would never marry a woman like me.

He went on saying cruel things up till the point when I turned on him and very politely informed him that I would infinitely prefer the 'Prince's harem' to the endless lifelong boredom of being married to someone like him. Then he became quite vicious and hissed at me – 'You'll pay for this Kitty. I'll make sure that you pay,' before he strode off in a huff.

I told Dickie about what A.B had said, when we were in bed together last night and he wasn't the least bit sympathetic. He said I oughtn't to have accepted that idiot's proposal in the first place and it was only to be expected. 'You can't spurn a man's ego by leaving him for another and expect him to take it lying down.'

So I asked him what he would do if I ever left him for another man. I only meant it as a joke but Dickie went very quiet and then looked at me with those unfathomable black eyes and told me in a voice that sent chills up my spine – 'I would kill you.' And I knew he meant it. He then proceeded to make love to me almost violently, something I had never encountered before but I didn't mind. It was very different from the gentle love making I have known with him. And it made me want him even more, if that's possible. There's never a dull moment whenever I'm with him. And that is what I love most about being with him.

Speaking about the unexpected, this morning just before he left my room, Dickie walked up to my closet and pulled out my red silk gown. He told me that he expected me to wear it this evening for dinner. I was too sleepy to argue, what can I do, the man doesn't let me sleep at night! I agreed but I wondered whether he going to choose what clothes I would wear from now on! But I learnt the reason for his command only later. There was a discreet knock on my door just as I was getting ready for dinner. The new amah (I've nicknamed her the 'raccoon' lately) opened the door to let in Dickie's most trusted Khidmatgar - Bahadur Singh. He came in with a large silver tray covered with a golden silk cloth and offered it to me along with a monogrammed note from Dickie that had two words printed on it – 'Wear it.' I lifted the cloth and gasped in astonishment. It was the most spectacular ruby necklace I've ever laid eyes on. Not that I've laid eyes on many, to begin with, but

I've certainly never seen anything like this. I asked the raccoon to help me put it on and she did, but with a sour face. I think she would've preferred putting a hangman's noose around my neck instead.

Before going in to join the others, I stopped by at the nursery to say goodnight to Rosie and Padma. Rosie was sweet and gushed about how beautiful I looked and little Padma wanted a story. Miss Martha just sat in one corner, giving me a disdainful look. If I started counting the disdainful looks I've been getting of late, from all over the place I'd run out of fingers and toes! Why can't people just allow other people to be happy? What is it about a sparkling happiness that seems to bring out the worst in these sad faced moralists? I can't help but feel sorry for them – having to go through life never experiencing love and wonder. And I can only hope that someday they too experience joy, the way I have, although someone like Angela probably won't know what joy is, even if it came and hit her in the face or did a little dance in front of her! I don't know why it should bother me though.

Anyhow, I created quite a sensation as I walked in to the main hall, sparkling like a Christmas tree! This necklace does rather have an effect on people. The men stared at me and the women looked on enviously. As I walked by I heard Mrs. Jenkins – some ICS chap's wife, whisper loudly to another plain looking woman standing next to her, 'Immorality seems to be paying rather well, these days!' and the other one replied with a start 'Oh, but it always has, my dear!' Jealous cats! They meant for me to hear it but I pretended as if I hadn't and sashayed past them over to where Dickie was. He *gave me a welcoming smile and put his hand on the small of my back in a proprietorial gesture and handed me his champagne flute. As I stood by him and sipped champagne, he whispered in my ears – 'I knew this was meant for you. You look like a Goddess.'*

Soon we were surrounded by a lot of people and I could see A.B and Angela huddled together in one corner looking quite glum. I suspect the necklace was Dickie's subtle way of keeping people like A.B in their place. A while later Angela made her way up to me and asked if we could have a word in private. I excused myself and we went out of the French windows on to the terrace. What she had to say to me is not worth repeating or writing about in this journal. But I did manage to tell her that if she felt so strongly about what I had done to A.B, she might as well marry him herself.

Chapter Twenty Three

Rachel smiled as she put down the journal. She was beginning to really like Kitty Riverton. The amah had come in earlier and switched on the lamps in her room. By now, it had become quite dark outside. She looked out of the window as lightening flashed across the sky over Dharanpore. While she had been reading, storm clouds had gathered and peals of thunder shook the air. She realised that she had only fifteen minutes before the dinner gong would sound. She got up and hurriedly dressed for dinner. As she picked out a well worn emerald green silk dress, she thought of Kitty's closet and her beautiful collection of clothes that almost made her wish she had gone on a shopping spree before coming out to India! The thought also reminded her to ask Jeremy if he had managed to send the wire to Inspector Parker regarding Kitty's legacy. She wondered if the Dharanpore post office was open on Sundays.

As if on cue, Jeremy walked in to the room in his dinner jacket and asked, 'Ready for dinner, darling?'

'I could eat a horse.'

'We'll try to keep you away from Riverton's polo ponies in that case. I've just been on a tour of the royal stables and the polo grounds.'

'Whatever for?'

'Well, you were off somewhere and the Colonel asked if I wanted to see the Prince at his polo practice and I agreed. He is rather good. Has a terrific polo handicap.'

'I haven't seen any horses about. Where is this polo ground?'

'It's just a five minute drive away. Right next to the elephant stables. We went in the Rolls. I'm beginning to see why the Colonel loves India so much. It's a charmed life.'

'Not for the starving millions, it isn't.'

'And we're planning to join the communist party, are we?'

'No, Jeremy. I don't know what it is, really. It all just seems so unreal to me. Being here in India in this great big Palace, the servants, the polo ponies, the elephant stables, the eight course meals, every luxury provided us...'

'And that is a problem because...?'

'I had this whole other picture of India in my head, you know, that of hunger, poverty and disease. And yet even when we drove past the villages on our way from the Dharanpore airfield, I saw these little boys chasing each other with glee and jumping into the pond naked. They seemed to be having a really great time. I wonder if we haven't been sold a pup with all those documentaries we saw of starving, famine ridden villagers.'

'No, my dear we haven't. Dharanpore is a very well run, and might I add, rich Royal State. It does not represent the rest of India. The Prince was telling me about all the developments his father has made, including a canal system from a large reservoir that ensures the crops get plenty of water even if the monsoon does a disappearing act, once every three years. The taxation laws are flexible, so farmers don't have to starve if there is a drought. He is also thinking of opening a few more textile mills and soap manufacturing factories, so that they can create more employment. They have already built schools and a few hospitals and they have plans to build more. All things considered, they seem to have got their act together over here.'

'Oh, that is interesting.'

'Yes and by the way, we just got news that massive rioting has broken out in Punjab, not very far from here and entire villages are burning. The Prince told me that he tries to see to it that he goes personally armed with a few sentries with rifles, to quell any nonsense of that sort before it gets worse, in his own State. But he too seems to be worried about what the future may bring. For now, people here are quite peaceful while the rest of northern India is burning.'

'I see. The Prince seems to be quite a man.'

'He is. Now, may we go for dinner, or would you prefer that we join the ranks of the starving millions?'

II

After dinner, Rachel asked Jeremy and the Colonel to come up for a small conference in her room. A walk would have been preferable but by the time they finished dinner it was raining cats and dogs. The electrical storm had led to a heavy cloudburst. As Jeremy and the Colonel made themselves comfortable in the armchairs, Rachel pulled up her study table chair towards the marble topped table and put a piece of white paper on it. As peals of thunder continued to join the howling wind and rain outside their window, she handed a pencil to him and asked the Colonel, if he remembered what the muddy footprints he had found near Kitty's body had looked like.

The Colonel was puzzled by her strange request but he made a rough sketch from his memory.

Then she addressed them both, 'I was right! This reinforces my theory that it was a person with a limp, on the right side to be precise. You see generally when one walks, footprints will be evenly placed one ahead of the other. In this case the feet seem to be together. Now if I had a limp in my right leg, I would walk like this,' she said, putting her left leg forward and then bringing her right leg forward to be by its side. Then she gingerly took another step with her left leg and brought her right leg to the same length but slightly behind the other. 'Now, if I were to walk normally, you wouldn't see both my feet so close together. My footprints would be like this,' she said, striding forward so one print was ahead of the other by the distance of a foot.

'Yes, I get it now. That's a nifty bit of leg work. So you are saying that it was a person with a limp. I don't remember anyone with a limp in the Palace at the time,' the Colonel said, looking nonplussed.

'Think harder, Colonel. It must have been Kitty's amah. Remember she was attacked by Sheba two nights before Kitty was killed? And the resulting fall made her limp. The Princess herself told me so. And now what Elliot told me today is beginning to make so much sense.'

'What did he tell you?' The Colonel asked.

She gave them both a brief of what Elliot had told her. The Colonel was livid.

'Why that little weasel, I'm going to skin him alive. Why couldn't he have told me this back then?'

Rachel responded, 'Perhaps because it was his word against the Princess' and he was scared of *precisely* this sort of a reaction from all sides.'

'He's a damned idiot. I would've hounded that bloody amah until she confessed and then it wouldn't be his word against anyone. We would have gotten to the bottom of this. I could have asked Charlie – our Political Agent, to take the case up to the Viceroy. The damned pernicious little fool.'

'We could still hound the amah, couldn't we?' Rachel asked.

Colonel Riverton sighed and said, 'The amah in question went back to her village in Punjab, the day before yesterday and has, in all likelihood, been burnt alive in the train by now. Oh, that bloody idiot.'

Rachel said, 'Then there's only one thing left to do – we'll have to make a clean breast of it to the Prince and ask him to confront the Princess.'

'I'm game. Let's do it right away,' the Colonel said, getting out of his armchair with a determined look.

Jeremy stopped them, 'Whoa! Wait on, both of you seem to be jumping the gun. Elliot didn't actually see the amah commit the crime. Have you considered the possibility that in her duty as a spy, she may have stumbled upon Kitty's body and gone to report it to the Princess?'

Rachel disagreed. 'Surely, the fact that the Princess panicked and packed the amah off to her village as soon as I wanted to question her, shows that she has something to hide? And what about this strange metallic object she handed over to the Princess?'

'There could be a number of explanations for both. Firstly, the amah may have wanted to be back with her family of her own accord, seeing that there is trouble brewing in Punjab. The metal thing could've been a bunch of keys for all you know. Elliot himself admits that he couldn't see much without his glasses.'

'What's your explanation for the fact that the Princess threatened him with dire consequences if he were to tell anyone about seeing what he did... apparently she even based her threats on Kitty's murder and the robbery.'

Jeremy answered evenly. 'Now there we do go into the realm of speculation – his word against hers. We know that Elliot has all kinds of paranoia. What if the Princess thought that he had caught the amah spying and she threatened him to stop him from revealing that? Is it possible that in his confused state, he misunderstood or blew the whole thing out of proportion in his mind, after learning the very next day that Kitty had been murdered and robbed?'

Colonel Riverton said, 'You do have a point there. I wouldn't put it past that bugger to make a mountain of a molehill! What do you suggest, we do?'

'For now, nothing. At least not until we have some more evidence to go upon. At this stage it's all based on hearsay and we'll just get their backs up for nothing. We know that the amah was there but we have no way of knowing if she was in fact the murderer. And I personally think, it'll be best if we wait till Arthur and Angela get here. They may have seen or heard something that didn't register as important at the time. Now with a lot more information to go on, and hopefully more eye witnesses, we may actually have a case worth taking to the Prince.'

Chapter
Twenty Four

The next morning dawned dewy fresh as the heavy downpour had cleared away the dust from the horizon. Rachel decided to take a small walk before breakfast. The air was crisp with the fragrance of wet earth and the Palace garden was charged with the sounds of a hundred bird and insect calls. To Rachel's mind, even the gnarled old trees looked bright and new with shiny clean leaves as if a hand from heaven had just reached down and planted them.

In a few hours, Arthur and Angela were due to arrive. She wanted to finish reading Kitty's journal before they did. But she realised that she was not alone in wanting to be out and about, as little Padma came running up to greet her with delight.

'Rachel, do you want me to give you flying lessons?'

'Not now, my dear. I've got to finish my reading.'

'Is it a storybook? Will you read me a story?'

'Well. It certainly is a story book of sorts but I doubt that I can read it out to you,' Rachel said, waving it at her with a smile. 'You see, Princess, it is someone's personal life story or a diary and I am reading it because I need to know more about this person.'

'Is it Kitty's diary?' The child asked with a clear gaze that filled Rachel with wonder at the child's preternatural ability.

'As a matter of fact, it is, but how did you know?'

'I used to sit with her sometimes, in the garden when she used to write in it, she showed me a picture of a tiger she had made. It was a funny picture!'

'Yes it is. And let me tell you a very funny story about a cat I once knew who looked exactly like that tiger Kitty drew,' Rachel said, as she proceeded to tell Padma all about King George.

They spent the next fifteen minutes talking and laughing till Nanny Rosie called her charge in for breakfast.

Before leaving Padma said, matter-of-factly, 'Kitty comes in my dreams sometimes.'

'Really and does she say anything?'

'Yes she says that I should be a pilot when I grow up. Last night she came and gave me a silver pencil. It was heavy. But of course it wasn't there anymore when I woke up. It was only a dream pencil. Okay, I have to go now,' she said, as she ran towards Nanny Rosie who waved at Rachel from a distance.

Rachel waved back at Rosie as she saw the little girl running back to the nursery windows. She glanced up and saw the Prince looking at her from an upstairs window. She waved at him too but he didn't wave back. He seemed to be lost in a world of his own.

Then it struck her with a force. She remembered the silver pencil she had inadvertently put in her skirt pocket. She had completely forgotten about it. She felt a distinct chill go up her spine. Was it possible that Kitty's spirit sent her a message that she wanted the thing back in her room? No, it couldn't be. She was just being paranoid. The child's dream must have been a bizarre coincidence. However, she had read somewhere that children were far more perceptive to beings and messages from the other side and made up her mind to go and replace it as soon as possible. A few words from Kitty's diary, floated into her mind – 'There are more things on heaven and earth, Horatio...'

Then she made her way to the orchid nursery and began reading;

I am really annoyed. Dickie's younger brother has been getting fresh with me. He tried to put his hands around my waist and came far too close for my comfort. I told Dickie about it and all he said was that Yuvraj was probably trying his luck with me. He even had the gall to tell me that it was only natural and that apparently, in India, good girls don't sleep with men they aren't married to. As if England is any different. Anyway I told him that was the wrong answer and that he had better have a little talk with his younger brother or else! 'Or else what?' He asked me and I told him that I would go back to England since it was evident that he had no intention of marrying me. I was livid and raved and ranted on for a while. He just stared at me for a while and just walked away without another word. Perhaps Arthur was right about him. What have I gotten myself into!

Rachel read a few more pages - there was more love making followed by an odd fight here and there. Rachel realised that Colonel Riverton had been right about the Prince once again. In all this time, he had not actually proposed marriage to Kitty even once. Or perhaps, he wanted to but Kitty hadn't lived long enough to hear the proposal. She read more of the diary till she reached the end. The last page read;

Angela has been quieter than usual. I suppose it has to do with the letter she received from home, this morning. As she read it at the breakfast table, her face went ashen and when I asked her what it was about, she hurriedly put it away and mumbled something about it being nothing and that she would tell me later.

When I cornered her later in the day, she hissed at me and told me she finally knew who Zephyr23 was! You could have knocked me down with a feather. Who would have guessed the pale-faced little snoop had been playing detective all along. Anyhow I don't see what she can do about it now. The war is over and the only sensible thing to do is to forget about it and move on with our lives. I told her as much. But seriously hat's off to her, she's managed to wheedle out this much information already. I am beginning to suspect that she does have brains after all – possibly far more than I've given her credit for in the past!

II

After lunch the Blackwell family arrived. They had a nanny with them who took the twins straight to the Palace nursery to be fed. Meanwhile, Colonel Riverton introduced Arthur and Angela to Jeremy and Rachel. Angela looked tired and harassed. She was a frumpily dressed woman in spectacles and Rachel had a hard time believing that she was related in any way to someone as flamboyant as Kitty. Arthur Blackwell on the other hand was exactly as she had pictured him. He was tall, thin lipped, with a moustache and had a slightly pompous air about him. He seemed to be developing a pot belly but looked like the sort of man who took a great deal of trouble to maintain his appearance. He seemed to be the kind of person who revelled in the company of other men in a 'for he's a jolly good fellow' kind of way that seemed superficial to her.

She was surprised to see that he and Jeremy seemed to be getting along, but then she realised that Kitty's diary had probably coloured her own judgement with a touch of bias against the couple. She had read more of Kitty's diary that morning and found that she didn't like the way either had treated Kitty after she had broken off her engagement. It was Angela's behaviour in particular that Rachel found to be more jarring of the two. Angela was her sister after all but there seemed to be no trace of sisterly love or comfort in any of her actions pertaining to Kitty. And yet it seemed odd to Rachel that Angela didn't waste any time in marrying the man, she so strongly disapproved of her sister rejecting.

They spent a few minutes talking and then the Colonel took them to meet the Prince and Princess in the royal wing.

III

Later that evening, Rachel had a chance to take a walk alone with Angela in the gardens and was at the receiving end of the latter's frustration at being back in India.

'God! I hate it here. I hated it back then and even more so now,' Angela said, kicking a pebble out of the way with her shoe.

'Then why did you come back?' Rachel queried.

'I had no choice! Arthur has got it into his head that we ought to be here, to help this investigation along. Although I don't see how our being here can help in any way. Kitty is dead and buried and if we couldn't figure out who killed her at the time, I don't see how we are going to do so now, two years later when the trail has gone quite cold.'

'I don't know Angela. Personally I think, sometimes it is easier to see things in retrospect.'

'I don't understand.'

'I'm not putting it very well. What I mean to say is that when the emotional charge is gone from an event or a situation, things tend to become clearer in the mind.'

'Well, they haven't gotten any clearer in mine. If anything, it's all slightly more muddled up in my head – the sequence of events and that sort of thing.'

'That's not nearly as important as what you felt, saw and heard during that time. Tell me, did Kitty have a lot of enemies?'

'It's hard to tell. She was very charming, good at games, a good horsewoman and an able shot which made her quite popular at house parties and such. Men loved her but she did face quite a bit of envy from women but that's only to be expected, I suppose. Her mere presence was enough to make most women cling on to their husbands for dear life. She had that sort of an effect on people.'

Rachel laughed, 'Yes, she also seems to have had a certain disregard for life and its set rules. I can see how that could be threatening to a lot of people.'

'Yes, you've hit the nail on the head. Kitty for all her brilliance could sometimes be mindless to the point of imbecility. But don't get me wrong, she was a very intelligent woman. She just lacked that moral code which tells us right from wrong.'

'But everybody's moral code is different, don't you think?'

'Well yes, to a point. And Kitty believed the same thing. She would often say that morals were for cattle and one person's floor was another person's ceiling. But I know that is not true beyond a point. Life teaches us right from wrong, in this world. It is what defines us as human beings.'

'I know what you mean. Killing someone, for example, is certainly wrong.'

'Really? I disagree. I think killing someone can be justified if one chooses to kill the root cause of harm or an impediment to a greater good. Arthur often says that if someone had the brains to assassinate Hitler at the right time, we could've prevented the awful things, he went on to do.'

'That is an interesting perspective. But please don't get me wrong. I am no closet fascist but to my mind, we all come here for a purpose and perhaps that was Hitler's purpose. To show us what evil can do. Killing anyone defeats the purpose of their existence, don't you think?'

'I can tell you that you are amongst a fraction of the population. Personally, I would have shot the man in a blink of an eye. There are limits to what one ought to be allowed to do in this world. Mass murder is not one of them.'

'Yet you would be ready to commit murder to prevent murder!'

'Certainly. Isn't that why countries go to war? It is always the intention behind an action that counts. When you do something for a greater good, even killing can be condoned.'

'I'm afraid, like the cartographers of old, I am bound to say that from here on, we tread on unchartered territory, dangerous seas where monsters may lurk.'

'Really, Rachel! I've never thought of philosophy as a monster. It is what gives us our true sense of identity.'

'Only to an extent but I suppose we can agree to disagree on that,' Rachel said with a smile. 'Tell me, Angela, were you fond of Kitty?'

'Yes to a point, I suppose I was. We were after all, sisters. But to be honest, as you can probably make out, we didn't have very much in common.'

Rachel smiled and found herself thinking that the sisters had more in common than they gave each other credit for. Single mindedness for one, apart from the courage to air their views on difficult subjects, without the fear of resulting repercussions.

There was something else she had wanted to ask Angela but had forgotten what it was. It suddenly resurfaced in Rachel's mind. She asked, 'I heard that you and Kitty had an argument on the night of her death. I don't mean to pry but can you tell me what it was about?'

'I daresay we did. We rarely saw eye to eye and often argued about things. And yes I remember we had words that night but I can't seem to remember what it was about. Probably the ungracious way that she treated Arthur.'

'Oh, I thought it may have something to do with a letter you received from home that morning. It's there in Kitty's diary.'

'Is it? I told you I'm all muddled in my head about the events of the day. Yes, you are right. I think it was about the news I received in the letter. Did the diary mention what it was about?'

'Not really, except for a mention of a 'Zephyr23'. I have no idea what it meant. Do you know?'

'Oh that – nothing important. It was a fanciful code name used by a SOE in the war.'

'The secret service?'

'MI6'

'I see and who was Zephyr23?'

'No one knew his real identity, just the code name. All I learned from the letter was that Zephyr 23 was the man responsible for betraying a crucial mission that my late fiancé - Jim Harding, had been a part of.'

'And you suspected that Kitty knew about this Zephyr23?'

'Yes, I suspected that she withheld the information from me all these years and I thought it rather unfair. But to be honest, it really has no connection with this investigation. I was just upset that she never shared it with me. It would have helped me find closure with Jim's death. But then Kitty could be so heartless sometimes.'

Rachel interjected gently, 'Or perhaps, in her way, she may have wanted to spare you the pain of knowing.'

'You know, in retrospect, I think you may be right about that,' Angela said with a sad smile.

Chapter Twenty Five

The next morning as they were having breakfast, Arthur spoke up. 'I think we ought to re enact what we were each doing, on the night of Kitty's murder. Nanny Rosie, Miss Martha and Colonel Riverton could be where they were at the time of her murder, say around one-thirtyish.'

'We'd all be in our rooms, in that case. I don't see how this will help,' Rosie said.

'It's an old tried and tested method, Nanny, to figure out where everyone was that night and it may even help you remember something vital you saw or heard which didn't seem important at the time,' Arthur said with conviction.

'If you say so, Mr. Blackwell,' she said, sounding unconvinced.

Arthur went on in his pompous style, 'Rachel, you could stay at the marble folly and be Kitty and Jeremy, you could be Elliot. Angela and I, will of course be ourselves.'

Mmm...must I?' Jeremy said, mimicking Elliot. 'I'm sorry I couldn't resist that,' he said with a smile, as Rachel shook her head at him in disapproval.

'Why can't Elliot be himself?' Miss Martha asked.

'Well I've been given to understand that he has a touch of nerves and he's a bit under the weather today. At any rate, I don't suppose he will be in any shape to do the kind of running about, he seems to have done, on the night in question. Jeremy on the other hand seems fit enough.'

At that moment, the Princess walked in followed by her Khidmatgar.

Arthur was the first to greet her with a startled, 'Oh, good morning, Your Highness.'

'Good morning Mr. Blackwell, ladies and gentlemen. I came by to see how you were all getting on. With the investigation, that is.'

There was silence as the others didn't know whether they were supposed to divulge the information of re-enacting the night of the murder.

Rachel spoke, 'Princess, I am so glad you are here. Saved me the long trek to your wing. I've been meaning to ask you something. Is it true that the amah I wanted to interview has been sent back to her native village in Punjab?'

'Yes and no,' she said with a smile. 'Let me clarify. Yes, I did inform her that you wanted to question her but she had far heavier things on her mind. These are difficult times for people whose families are in Punjab. You must have heard about the terrible situation there. And no, I didn't send her back. She went of her own accord to be with her family in this time of turmoil. She has children and grandchildren back there and she was naturally very concerned for their safety. If all goes well, she will be back within a week. I have promised them all sanctuary here at Dharanpore.'

'Thank you for letting me know, Princess, and if I may say so, that was a very kind gesture on your part.'

'It is not kindness on my part, Lady Markham, but my duty to stand by my people in times like these,' the Princess responded in all seriousness.

II

Half an hour later, the Princess had returned to her wing and they had begun re-enacting the events leading to Kitty's death and Rachel found herself wandering about inside the marble folly. The Sun streamed in and in the light of day, it was a beautiful place with its polished white marble floor and carved pillars. The garden surrounded it on all sides. It was a tranquil place. If she hadn't known any better, she would have never guessed in a million years, that this peaceful space had witnessed a brutal murder just a few years ago.

It was a warm day and she crossed the length of the folly to the shaded side. She reached one of the pillars at the end and decided to sit on the floor with her back resting against it. It was cool to touch. She fancied this was close to the spot, which Colonel Riverton had pointed to, when he had shown them where Kitty's body had been found. She could hear birds chirping in the trees and the occasional call of the peacock. It was an idyllic place for day dreaming and after a heavy breakfast she was beginning to feel a bit drowsy. To keep awake she began to hum a song to herself. After a while the ditty she was humming faded on her lips, as she dozed off.

The next thing she knew, someone was shaking her awake. It was Jeremy. He was bending over her and there was concern in his voice, 'Rachel, are you alright? What happened?'

'Nothing. I think I dozed off for a bit. Ouch!' She exclaimed as she cut her hand against a jagged edge at the bottom of the pillar, in her attempt to get up, using it as a support.

'That's strange – the carving is not supposed to have sharp edges,' he said, getting down to inspect the bottom of the pillar. 'It looks like the marble has chipped off here. Do be careful.'

'It's only a small cut. I'll be fine,' Rachel said sucking on her little finger.

'Well, come along, we've all been waiting for you in the morning room. Everybody has gathered there to discuss the outcome of our little experiment.'

III

As no one had any fresh inputs, the experiment had not yielded much. They dispersed after a while to resume their respective activities for the day. Rachel was still feeling sleepy and decided to head to her room for a mid morning nap. The moment she entered she knew something was amiss. Her satchel was lying open on the bed and the study table was a mess as if someone had quickly rifled through it and not bothered to put things back in their place.

She instinctively ran towards her bed to check if Kitty's diary was in its hiding place under the mattress. The bed sheets were untidily tucked back. The diary was gone. Her drowsiness vanished in an instant. Next, she checked in her satchel for Kitty's room key. She emptied out the contents on the bed. The key was gone as well. She went to look for Colonel Riverton and Jeremy to inform them about this new development.

She found them in the courtyard along with Arthur Blackwell.

She joined them and said excitedly, 'The experiment wasn't a total failure. Someone ransacked my room, at their convenience, while we were at it. Whoever it was, managed to purloin Kitty's room key and her diary from my room!'

The three men spoke all at once.

'Of all the ...'

'You don't say!'

'Bloody hell!'

Rachel smiled, 'So you see, the experiment was a resounding success. I think we are closer to finding out who has something to hide and it narrows our circle of suspects a bit.'

'Eh, what?'

'Well, we can safely assume that it was someone who knew that I would be away from my room for some amount of time and took the chance to rifle through my things.'

'Yes, I can see that but it could have been anyone in the Palace.'

'No. You are mistaken. Only the people in that room knew for sure that they would not be disturbed during the search. So I think we can safely rule out the Prince, the Princess and Elliot from our list of suspects.'

'I don't see how you can rule out the Princess. She may have overheard our plans. She came in quite unexpectedly this morning,' Arthur Blackwell said.

'No, I very much doubt that she would be listening with her ear to the door with a Khidmatgar in tow. No, it was not her.'

'What are you suggesting? Are you suspecting one of us?' Blackwell asked indignantly.

'Never mind what I suspect, Mr. Blackwell,' she said and then turning towards Colonel Riverton, 'For now, I think it would be best if you got the second key to Kitty's room, Colonel. I remember that you did mention there was another,' Rachel said. 'I want to see if anything has vanished from her room.'

'Er... ah, yes. There is another key with the cleaning amah. But they already got her diary. Wasn't that what they were after in the first place?' he asked, nonplussed.

'No. They were obviously after something else in her room. If it was just the diary they were after, they wouldn't have bothered to take her room key as well. Don't you see, there must be something else? And it could be something we overlooked as unimportant. It could be the vital clue to solving this whole thing. Oh, do get me the second key. I have a fairly good memory and I will notice if there's anything missing from her room as well.'

Chapter
Twenty Six

Half an hour later, Rachel was going through Kitty's room with a fine tooth comb. The Colonel had gasped in astonishment as he turned the key and they had walked in. Here, the evidence that the room had been rifled was all the more evident. The wardrobe doors were left open. The wardrobe itself was in a mess, as if someone had pulled down most of her dresses in an attempt to find something. Even her bed and study table had not been spared. The sheets had been ripped off and the pen stand had been emptied on to the desk. The drawers were pulled out and their contents emptied on to the floor. It was obvious to Rachel that someone had acted out of desperation and had run out of time to put things back in their place.

Jeremy looked up from the floor near the study table, where he was sorting out Kitty's papers and said, 'Well, whatever they were looking for, they didn't find it at the desk. Her papers are all messed up but they all seem to be here. To the best if my knowledge, I don't think anything is missing from here.'

Rachel answered absentmindedly, 'Right, good for you, darling. I can't say the same with any amount of surety. I don't think I would know if something is missing from her wardrobe. She had a number of dresses and I don't know if any one in particular is missing.'

'Really? I find that hard to believe,' Jeremy said with a grin.

'Oh, wait a minute! Her red silk gown seems to be missing!'

'Atta girl! That's more like it.'

'No, no, it's not. It's right here, under some other dresses at the foot of the wardrobe. What an awful way to treat such beautiful clothes. I could kill the person who did this!' She said, as she reverentially started dusting the clothes and putting them back on their hangers.

After arranging everything back the way it was on their first visit, Rachel sighed and said, 'I suppose I was wrong. Nothing seems to be missing from her room and yet I'm certain they were looking for something in particular.'

'That's rather obvious, isn't it, darling?' Jeremy said with a raised eyebrow.

'Yes of course. What I meant to say is that it has got to be something small that they knew was here and yet they couldn't find it even after turning her room upside down. I wonder what it could have been.'

'Something small, you say?'

'Most definitely, otherwise why would they search under the sheets and amongst her clothes? And if it was something sizeable, we would have noticed it on our first visit and consequently its disappearance.'

'Yes, I agree with you there but the moot question remains – what on earth were they searching for?'

II

In the evening, Jeremy shared the telegram they had received from Inspector Parker, in response to their queries about Kitty's legacy. It stated quite plainly that she had been left a sum of three hundred pounds a year and the cottage. Kitty had not sold it. In any case, its market value was about seven hundred pounds.

That night, after dinner, Rachel felt inordinately tired. She couldn't keep her eyes open. She excused herself from the dining room and went to bed early. She fell asleep as soon as her head hit the pillow but her deep sleep was disturbed by a recurring dream, which took on a nightmarish quality. She was desperately searching for something in the mist and she could feel that someone invisible with cold clammy hands was trying to push her forward. There were voices floating around her, as if carried on an eerie breeze;

> *It could have been anyone in the Palace...*
>
> *The fires of hell are her punishment...*
>
> *You have no idea what you're up against...*
>
> *She gave me a silver pencil...*

Philosophy gives us our true sense of identity...

I don't see why she had to go to the zenana...

Had I known, I would have shot her myself...

Then there was a sound of a loud bang. Rachel shot up from her pillow suddenly very alert and aware of clear and present danger. A stream of light came in from the corridor through the doorframe. Her room door was slightly ajar. Then she saw a shadow outside in the corridor as her door closed with a click. The room was in pitch darkness once more. Someone had been in her room while she slept and had left just before she awoke. She reached out to her bedside lamp and fumbled for the switch. She found it and put it on. The darkness dispelled, she saw that chair near the study table had been knocked down. Whoever it was had come back to search her study table again. In the process this person had knocked the chair down by mistake and fled in panic with the resulting noise of the chair hitting the floor. That must've been the banging sound that had woken her in the first place.

She knew there was no point in trying to chase this person. By the time she would put her dressing gown on, to follow suit, he or she would have disappeared down one of the many connecting corridors in the Palace. The place was a labyrinth! Her head felt heavy. It didn't worry her anymore.

Nothing did, as the realisation dawned on her that she *knew* exactly what this person had been searching for! In a blinding flash, she finally knew how Kitty had been murdered. Now it was just a question of trying out the murder weapon and laying a small trap to catch the killer.

After that she would go to the Dharanpore post office and see if she could make a telephone call to Inspector Parker and ask him to wire her some information.

III

The next morning, Rachel asked Jeremy to help her tie a bandage on her wounded hand.

He sounded concerned as he said, 'If the cut has gotten worse, you may want to show it to Dr. Saunders, darling. After all we don't want you catching some strange tropical infection.'

'Don't be silly, darling. The cut has almost healed, see? I need the bandage for something else.'

'Eh?'

'I'm going to use this hand like a worm to catch a fish. A slippery one at that.'

'Eh, what?'

'Never mind, Jeremy. I'll explain it all later in the evening. Do be a dear and bandage it for me.'

Fifteen minutes later, she picked up some notepapers and a pencil and headed towards the school room. She found Elliot there and asked him if he could help her write a note to Miss Martha and Nanny Rosie. She waved her hand bandaged hand in front of him and said, 'I can't write properly. That cut I got the other day seems to be worse. Sorry to be a nuisance.'

'Not at all. What is it you wish me to write?'

'Dear Miss Martha & Nanny Rosie, we request the pleasure of your company post dinner at nine thirty pm tonight, in the Palace library. We will be discussing some important matters pertaining to the investigation. Yours faithfully, Jeremy & Rachel.'

'That's interesting. Am I invited as well?'

'Of course you are! How silly of me not to have mentioned it before. You see, the case is solved and all the players must be present for the revelation.'

'How extraordinary! Are you saying you've found out everything?'

'Certainly.'

'It isn't going to go down very well with the royals but it will be most interesting to see how they handle your accusations.'

'Oh, I wouldn't worry so much, if I were you. I shan't be hurling accusations at them. Quite the opposite, in fact. I'm sure it will all turn out fine in the end. Well, I must trot along and find Miss Martha now. Thanks so much for your help, Elliot,' Rachel said, leaving behind a very puzzled man.

Next she found both Miss Martha and Nanny Rosie in the nursery. Nanny Rosie gave her a harried greeting and then shouted over her shoulder, 'Princess Padma! Please stop putting peas up their noses. Oh God! Do excuse me, Lady Markham. I've got my hands full with the royal children and the Blackwell twins on top of that.'

As she left to chase after the children, Rachel repeated the note writing process with Miss Martha and had her write a similar note addressing Angela and Arthur.

After that she found Teji Singh in the hall and requested him to guide her to Angela's room. She knocked and heard Angela say, 'Come in.'

Rachel entered and found that she was still in bed. She greeted her, 'Good morning, Angela. You look a bit fagged out. Didn't you get enough sleep last night?'

'It's the twins. They refused to go to bed and the nanny and I were up till all hours trying to get them to sleep.'

'Oh! I'm sorry,' Rachel said with a smile, as she sat in a chair by her bed. 'Having twins must mean double trouble.'

Angela grasped her arm and said in a harassed voice, 'Take it from me, Rachel. Don't have children! At any rate if you are foolish enough to have them, don't travel with them. It's simply ghastly.'

Rachel said, 'Dear me, Jeremy and I haven't given it much thought. I suppose I shall heed your advice if we ever do! Angela, dear, I need a smallish favour. Could you write out a small note to the Prince and Princess on my behalf? I'll get the blotter from the desk.'

Chapter Twenty Seven

At nine thirty at night, they had all gathered in the library. The attendees included Colonel Riverton, Angela and Arthur Blackwell, Sushanto Bose, Miss Martha, Nanny Rosie, Elliot Wilkins, Jeremy and of course Rachel. The only people missing were the two royal couples and Dr. Saunders. There was a buzz in the room and a sense of expectation hung over everyone.

Rachel addressed those present. 'Thank you all for coming. We will wait for the others to join but meanwhile please make yourselves comfortable.'

As soon as she said it, the doors opened and the Khidmatgar announced the arrival of the Prince Ravindra Richard and Princess Uma Devi. They were followed by Prince Yuvraj Dharan and Princess Tara Devi.

As the Prince walked past her, he said, looking at Rachel, 'Rumour has it, that you've solved the case. I'd be most interested to know who was behind the murder and the robbery.'

'Quite right, your highness. All will be revealed shortly. As soon as Dr. Saunders gets here.'

As if on cue, the Khidmatgar announced the arrival of the doctor.

He came in and said, 'Hello, everyone.' Then turning towards the royal couple, he nodded, 'Your Highness. Sorry to have kept you all waiting but had a last minute emergency. Had to amputate an infected leg. Last stage of gangrene, pus everywhere. Came as soon as I chopped it off. Why, hello Arthur, it's good to see you again old chap,' he said, as crossed the room in large strides and held his hand out to greet him. Rachel nearly laughed out loud as she saw Arthur Blackwell's expression of muted revulsion, as he reluctantly held out his hand to shake the doctor's, like a shrinking violet.

Dr. Saunders gave him a vigorous hand shake as he simultaneously patted the man on his back. 'Doing well, I see. Quite the married man now. By the looks of it, wife's been feeding you rather well,' he said, poking Blackwell's pot belly.

Arthur gave a wan smile and murmured something apologetic. He was trying to squirm out of the doctor's grasp.

Rachel came to his rescue and said, 'Right, Dr. Saunders, let's all settle down now and get to the business at hand, shall we?'

'Certainly, my dear, certainly!'

They were all seated in a semi circle and Rachel stood facing them.

'To begin with, I'd like to thank you all for being here tonight. Ever since Jeremy and I arrived here at the Palace, you all have shown us nothing but kindness. But now I have the unpleasant task of unmasking the truth and revealing the evil behind the events that took place two years ago. The truth will shock some of you and hurt others in this room but what can I say? It has to be done. As Dr. Saunders put it so well at our earlier meeting - that if you must take off plaster from a wound, you might as well do it quickly.'

'The suspense is killing me. Who was behind Kitty's death?' Angela asked.

Rachel continued, 'Before I get to that, I need to get something off my chest. This was a complicated case as it did not involve one but two crimes. The first of course was Kitty Riverton's murder and the second, the theft of the fabulous ruby. Now going by logic everyone believed that both crimes were committed by the same person or persons acting in tandem. However, I am here to tell you with a great deal of certainty, that is not the case here. There were two sets of disconnected perpetrators. I realised early on that it would be difficult, if not impossible to solve such a case using 'horse sense' or 'logic' and so I followed my intuition instead and listened to what a child had to say.

Yes, Princess, it was your daughter who first let me on to the real clue that cracked the case wide open. She spoke of a dream in which Kitty handed her a heavy silver pencil. Till such time it never occurred to me that it had any bearing on this case at all. Even at the time, when she told me about her dream, it did not register. The importance of it dawned on me late last night when my room was searched for a second time. You see, I realised then that it was the only thing missing from Kitty's room because I had inadvertently put in my skirt pocket. Thereafter, things started becoming clearer suddenly.'

The Prince asked, 'So let me get this. You are basing your findings in a murder investigation on a child's dream?' He looked at her queerly, trying to figure out if he had heard her correctly. Even Colonel Riverton was looking at her with his mouth open as if he was convinced that she had lost her marbles.

She answered, 'Yes. Yes. That and the can of worms it opened thereafter. I know it all sounds a bit dodgy right now but do hear me out.' She noticed that people were looking embarrassed and giving each other side glances as she spoke.

'We are all ears. Go on, so what happened after the child's dream,' Dr. Saunders said, looking at her with an amused expression. She could see he had visions of making her his new psychiatric project.

'Alright! I suppose I've confused you all enough. So let me go about it backwards.'

'Oh, yes. That would not be confusing at all!' Dr. Saunders guffawed.

'What I mean is that there were two crimes committed that night. I'll talk about the lesser of the two now – the jewel robbery.'

'Go on,' Colonel Riverton prodded.

'There was no robbery,' Rachel said simply.

'Ah!' Dr. Saunders was thoroughly enjoying himself by now.

Except for that one exclamation from him, there was complete silence in the room. You could hear a pin drop. A few moments later, Rachel who was standing quite close to the Colonel, could hear him muttering under his breath – something about having Chief Inspector Harrow's hide.

She smiled at him and then looked straight at the Princess. 'Will you tell them or would you rather I did, Princess?'

The Princess looked at her coldly and said, 'I don't know what you're talking about. I've had enough of this farce. When you really come up with the right answers, you can call for me.' She said, getting out of the armchair, in a move to leave.

Rachel spoke with a glint of steel in her voice, 'Sit down, Your Highness. It was your spy, the amah who stumbled upon Kitty's body in the marble folly. She then purloined the necklace from the dead girl and handed it over to you at the zenana. There is an eye witness, I can call upon, should the need arise.'

'I have never heard such gibberish in all my life! Who is your eye witness? Elliot Wilkins? A man known to be a thief? I suppose you never considered the possibility that he stole it himself and concocted this whole story to protect himself from being found out?'

'In that case, if you did not threaten him into silence and his story is not true, you would have had no interaction with him on the night in question. So how could you possibly zero in on Mr. Wilkins as an eye witness so quickly? I'm afraid, Princess, you've just tripped in your self-made trap.'

'Rubbish!' The Princess hissed. 'You'll accuse me of murder next. I refuse to be accused of such nonsense by a self proclaimed amateur detective who has no basis to make such accusations... '

The Prince interrupted her flow, in a voice like a whip, 'Uma!'

It had the magical effect of quietening the Princess down and she sat back with a sigh.

Rachel turned to the Prince and said, 'I am sorry Your Highness, but you did hire us to uncover the truth and the truth is that the necklace left the Palace in your luggage the very next day. The day you left for Bombay to attend the meeting of the Chamber of Princes. That's why although a thorough search was conducted, the necklace was not found. I had an interesting conversation the other day with your ADC – Mr. Bose. And if I'm not mistaken, the million pounds the State collected in insurance must have came in rather handy for the State exchequer. I hear new schools, hospitals and textile mills are in the pipeline. Not to mention that if ever privy purses are taken away by the Indian government, you will have a star ruby worth a million pounds that a lot of private collectors around the globe, would give their eye-teeth for. Indeed, a personal security blanket which the newly formed Government of India can no longer lay claim to.'

There was a hush around the room.

The Prince finally spoke, 'That is quite an interesting theory and never mind if the Princess and I agree with it or not. But we did also hire you to find out who killed Kitty Riverton. Your findings on that will be of greater interest to me.'

'Certainly, Your Highness. I am coming to that now.'

She paused for a moment and then continued, 'You see, never before have I come across a situation where one individual was equally loved and hated by various people in so many different ways. Kitty Riverton was the sort of person who seemed to have brought out the best and worst in the people she interacted with, or indeed, even had a passing interaction with. Starting with her own family – her father and sister.'

'What?' Colonel Riverton asked indignantly.

'Well, yes, Colonel. Both you and Angela disapproved of her behaviour intensely and there was a strong enough motive there, to stop her at any cost from making a huge mistake. The family honour was at stake.'

'Are you suggesting I murdered my daughter?'

'No, I am just pointing out that you had a motive, as did other people. Arthur Blackwell for example, who Kitty had unceremoniously cast aside a few days prior to getting killed.'

'Well, I'll be dashed!' Blackwell spoke up. 'It was a blessing in disguise. She would have made me a terrible wife.'

'In retrospect, perhaps. You certainly didn't seem to see it that way back then. You even threatened her with dire consequences.'

'I must've lost my temper. Heat of the moment and all that. I'm not proud of it but I didn't mean any harm and I certainly didn't kill her!'

'Yes. I know you didn't. Other people had stronger motives. The Princess of course had the strongest motive to get her out of the way before any lasting damage could be done. The fact that her husband gifted Kitty the Pride of Dharanpore undoubtedly set the alarm bells off, didn't they, Princess?'

'I have nothing to say. This is a waste of our time. Do you know who killed her or not?'

'Yes I do. But as I said in the beginning, there were two different crimes. And while I do believe that you employed a spy to keep an eye on Kitty, I do not believe that you killed her.'

'Thank God for small mercies!'

'Yes, well. I also know that Miss Martha hated everything that Kitty represented and for a while I wondered if she had anything to do with her death.'

Miss Martha said in a shaky voice, 'You cannot be serious, Lady Markham. I am a God fearing Christian and I would never kill anyone.'

'Yes. I realised that whatever the provocation, you would not break the commandment – 'Thou shalt not kill'. But apart from you, to my mind, Elliot was a suspect too. He was in love with Kitty and his motive could have been a disproportionate sense of jealousy when she chose to ignore him for another.'

Elliot stammered, 'Bbb...but surely, you aren't suggesting I killed her.'

'No, merely pointing out that each one of you, well most of you, in this room today had a motive but the crime was committed by one person and one person only. You see from the beginning, the greatest puzzle was the murder weapon. I also heard different accounts of what people heard and saw that night. Two people spoke about being woken up by a loud noise – a door banging somewhere. As firearms were positively ruled out, given the size of the wound, no one thought it could be anything else. In reality, it was this.'

Rachel took the silver pencil out of her pocket, aimed it in the air and pulled back a tiny button. There was a large popping sound followed by a resounding bang and smoke issued from the back end of the pencil.

She went on to explain, 'I received a telegram earlier today from a friend in the British intelligence who gave me details about this weapon. It was issued to SOE's – for those present who don't know what that means, SOE is an abbreviation for 'Special Operations Executives' or British secret agents and spies during the war.'

She stopped to pull out the telegram from her pocket and read it aloud. 'Called the propelling pencil pistol. Stop. 6.35mm cartridge inserted by unscrewing the end. Stop. Casing contains a spring loaded hammer to fire the cartridge. Stop. Trigger is released by pulling button back to fire. Stop. Tiny but deadly at close quarters. Stop.'

Dr. Saunders came forward and held out his hand. Rachel handed him the deadly pencil. From her skirt pocket she took out some tiny cartridges. She handed one over to him.

'I found these in Kitty's vanity case along with her trinkets, so I know that the gun belonged to her and that she was not only a pilot but also an SOE during the war.'

Dr. Saunders interrupted her, 'Yes, by Jove. The size certainly fits. I am going to do some tests before I can confirm your theory though.'

'By all means, Doctor. I don't mean to come across as smug but I can guarantee that you will find that this is the murder weapon. It was placed in Kitty's mouth as she lay prostrate and possibly unconscious in the marble folly and then the murderer fired. At such close quarters there was no chance of missing. Fact is, the bullet went through her head with such force that it chipped the marble off one of the pillars right behind where she lay. I know because I cut my hand on its jagged edge yesterday.'

Colonel Riverton spoke, 'I had no idea Kitty was a spy. Did you know, Angela?'

Angela remained silent. Rachel responded for her. 'Yes Angela knew. And I suspect she also guessed towards the end that Kitty was a double agent during the war, didn't you?'

Angela answered softly, 'Yes, she went rogue towards the end. She sold secrets pertaining to the number of military aircrafts and miscellaneous information regarding the base, to the other side.'

Rachel said, 'She did more than that. Kitty was the one who betrayed the mission in which, your fiancé – Jim

Harding and a few others lost their lives behind enemy lines. Kitty was Zephy23, wasn't she? And you killed her when you found out that she was responsible for Jim's death. She had to pay for it in the end, and it was up to you; to see to it, that she did.'

'Jim and the others weren't killed outright, Rachel. I know that Jim was captured behind enemy lines, interrogated for 72 hours and tortured to death. Only one out of the nine SOE's on that mission survived to tell the tale. And to think my sister – Kitty was responsible for sending our boys to their certain gruesome death. She knew what their fate would be. All this for what? Just money? She was ruthless. Jim was her friend too, you know.'

'She wasn't the only ruthless one. You killed her in cold blood too.'

'I was doing a national service. You know what we do to double agents?'

'Yes but I am also aware that there is a division that handles the trials for rogue spies and war criminals. You could have given this information to them and they would have conducted a trial. There was no need to take the law in to your own hands.'

'Yes there was. I could not have proven anything. You see, only I knew beyond a shadow of a doubt that she was Zephyr 23.'

'I don't understand.'

'Just after the war started we were reading this article on how SOE's were recruited with the most extraordinary names. There was one called Blunderbus18! Kitty had remarked at the time, how positively awful that sounded and she had said that if she ever became an SOE, she would call herself something romantic like Zephyr23. I distinctly remember because I had asked her what was so romantic about that - and weren't they ugly little biplanes used in the previous war? She had laughed and told me, 'No, you silly girl. Zephyr is the name given to the western wind which ushers in a lovely light spring with the early summer breezes that it brings.' Wind indeed! She was more like a tropical hurricane that destroyed everything in its wake!'

Rachel said, 'Yes, I can see where you're coming from. But something set you off. Something in that letter. The one you got on the morning of the fateful day.'

'Yes, the letter I got that morning was forwarded to me by Aunt Dorothea. It was from Jim's friend, Peter who was the only SOE to survive that mission and in the letter he mentioned that he had finally had a breakthrough. He had inside information that they were betrayed by a double agent whose real identity was yet unknown but operated under the code name Zephyr23. Imagine my surprise! It was too much of a coincidence. Except, it wasn't. All the pieces of the puzzle suddenly seemed to fit and the resulting picture was not pretty. Jim had divulged the details of his mission to both Kitty and me.

I knew then with certainty that Kitty had betrayed him, knowing full well what they would do to him at the other end. And for what? For the love of money! Here she was strutting about complacently, flaunting the frivolous things she had bought with his blood money. It was unbearable. I was furious and I confronted her the same day. She mocked me. She said the war was over and it was high time I stopped mooning over this 'fellow'.

I don't quite know what came over me after that. When she went for her bath I took her pencil pistol. I methodically took out and loaded the cartridge. She had shown me how it worked and I knew where she kept the cartridges. She was inordinately proud of her little pistol and would joke about it to me, saying that her pen was in fact mightier than a sword!'

I asked her out for a walk that night. Once we reached the folly, I picked up father's walking stick that I had kept hidden behind a pillar, sometime before and hit her with it. She fell unconscious. You know the rest.'

'Yes, I do, and I also know that Arthur helped you, in covering up your crime. If it weren't for him, you would not have had an alibi for the time of her death,' Rachel answered simply.

'Yes well, now you know. What are you going to do to me? To us?' Angela asked her.

'Me? Nothing. I was hired to find out the truth and that is what I've done. Now, I suppose it is up to the rest of you in this room. Or more specifically, His Highness. You are on his territory and the murder was committed here. So in effect, as the head of the State and ruling Monarch, he gets to decide upon your fate.'

Angela looked about the room in panic. Colonel Riverton had his head in his hands. Arthur Blackwell had gone a peculiar shade of grey. Everyone else was staring at the Prince, waiting with baited breath. The Prince did not so much as, glance at Angela. He was looking intently at Rachel with an unfathomable expression. Slowly and deliberately he began to speak.

'I salute you, Rachel Markham. I think I owe you an apology. We all do. For I know, I am not the only one in this room who underestimated your abilities. You have a certain, how shall I put it, *savoir faire* in unmasking the truth. It must be a divine gift since it comes so naturally to you.' Rachel didn't know how to respond and remained silent.

He then turned to Angela and spoke, 'Mrs. Blackwell, the provocation may have been great but I am sure you will see that I cannot personally condone the murder of one of my guests and indeed a close friend, in my own Palace. I could approach the Home Office in England and ask them to intervene as you are a British subject, as was Kitty and lay the facts of the case before them. However, you are also a friend and a guest in my home. My three thousand year old cultural heritage will not allow my conscience to do so. You are free to go.'

Angela was in tears. Arthur Blackwell spoke. 'Oh, Your Highness – you are kindness personified. Thank you for saving us! I thank you on behalf of our little children as well...'

The Prince cut him short before he could go any further. He spoke in an even voice, 'Mr. Blackwell, there is no need to thank me. Do not be under the mistaken impression that you and your wife have gotten away with murder. We have a saying in India that you may escape the law of the land but you will be answerable to a higher court, where no crime goes unpunished. We call it the law of karma.' With that he got up and left the room.

II

Colonel Riverton, Sushanto Bose and Dr. Saunders wanted to know more. They stayed back in the library with Jeremy and Rachel, after the others had left.

Colonel Riverton spoke, 'How did you know it was Angela?'

'I suppose when it dawned on me that the murder weapon was the pencil pistol, I realised that Kitty had to have been shot when she was lying down. The cut on my hand from the marble pillar reassured me that I was on the right track. That meant that someone would have hit her, rendering her unconscious before shooting her. Now I also remember she had a bruise on the right side of her forehead, which essentially pointed to the fact that she was hit from the front, as the assailant had to be facing her. That also made it obvious that this person was left handed. I conducted a little note writing experiment this morning to be sure and rule out the other two main suspects.'

'Yes, Angela is left handed. But Arthur could have just as easily manipulated her into committing this crime.'

'No, Arthur helped her cover up the crime and gave her an alibi. I think he followed them to the marble folly and saw what she had done. He is an ICS man and is trained to make split second decisions. He then took the murder weapon and kept it with him. He even gave her an alibi for the time of death.'

Jeremy who had been a mute spectator all this while, spoke up, 'All that's very well but you are getting ahead of the story. What I want to know is what put you on to them in the first place?'

'That's easy, Jeremy - our rooms being ransacked. I realised it was Arthur who suggested the whole re-enactment thing. I think his idea was to retrieve the murder weapon before anyone found out. Luckily it was on me, in my skirt pocket when they made the search. I think they came all the way to Dharanpore just for that.'

Sushanto Bose asked, 'If it was that important, why on earth, hadn't they gotten rid of it back then?'

'He did try. Two days after the murder, he thought he would hide it in the safest place possible – Sheba's cage. Even if the entire Palace was searched, no one was likely to look there! But what he hadn't accounted for was the fact that leopards are highly territorial animals. He let her out of the cage but she didn't fancy him entering it. I think she pounced on him before he could dig a hole and bury the pencil. But once Dr. Saunders gave the verdict that the murder weapon could not have been a firearm they were relieved. Angela had then taken it back from Arthur and hidden it in the safest place she could think of – in Kitty's pen stand!'

Dr. Saunders asked, 'How did you begin to suspect that Kitty had been a spy?'

'Inspector Parker wired us giving us the details of the legacy from her maternal aunt. Once we knew that the legacy left to her was a pittance and that she had not sold the cottage, I suspected something was amiss. Her own pay could not possibly cover her expenses, it was just a matter of putting two and two together. Pardon me, Colonel, but the thought had crossed my mind that she may have been in the oldest profession in the world! But the contents of her diary told me otherwise. It was clear to me that Kitty had been sexually innocent up until she was seduced by the Prince. That left me with no other choice but to explore the notion that she had been a spy. She was certainly in a good position to be one. And the pay must've been her motivation. The war had played havoc on everybody's nerves. I think Kitty just got tired of not having the things she wanted and money was the one thing that could give her whatever she desired. I don't really think she knew what she was getting into. You see, I think, it may have started out small and then snowballed in to something that she had no control over.'

Epilogue

Within twenty four hours of the revelation, Arthur and Angela Blackwell packed up and left with their children for Bombay. The Prince had very kindly allowed them the use of his chartered airplane. They spent a few days in Bombay before catching their ship to Hong Kong as planned. Rachel and Jeremy never heard from them again.

The Prince and the Princess left the day after for Delhi for talks with the Government. Princess Padma got to accompany them and she was over the moon that the pilot allowed her into the cockpit and even gave her the control of the joystick for a while. She was flying a real plane and she couldn't wait to tell Kitty the next time she came in her dream. Nanny Rosie told little Padma that she wasn't sure if Kitty would continue to come so often in her dreams, now onwards, because her soul was finally at rest.

Elliot Wilkins put in his papers and decided to travel through South Asia for a while. He had an idea that he wanted to see Borneo and China. And he reassured Rachel when she voiced her concerns that he had enough saved up to last him easily for two to three years. He even hinted that he didn't mind earning his way through his journey. He told her that he had an idea that he would write about his travels. If someone had informed her then that he would go on to becoming a world famous author and travel writer within a span of three years, Rachel would have laughed her head off. But Elliot was set on changing his destiny from 'mouse to man' as he put it. And the determined glint in his eyes gave Rachel a hint that he would go far.

Rachel and Jeremy wanted to see more of India before getting on their ship. Their passage home was still three and a half weeks away. Rachel was rather keen on seeing the Taj Mahal but they were dissuaded to travel up north by all, owing to the volatile situation there. She was disappointed but Colonel Riverton suggested that they had just about enough time to see something of South India. He informed them that he himself was in a dire need of a holiday and decided to accompany them to Ootacamund – a scenic hill station, high up in the Nilgiri Hills. Ooty, as the place was popularly christened had been the summer capital of the Madras Presidency.

Jeremy and Rachel met their first herd of wild elephants on the road to Ooty and fell in love with the large tea estate that they stayed in. They enjoyed the hospitality and company of the Hendersons – a British couple who had decided to stay on in India and run their estate. They had a wonderful time playing golf and visiting places of interest nearby. They spent their evenings at Ooty club. Finally, Rachel got to see what life on an Indian tea estate was like. She had heard so much about it from the novelist Dennis Hawthorne at her uncle's home – Rutherford Hall. Before they knew it, their time was up and they had to head back, to board their ship from Bombay.

They boarded the RMS Artemis on their journey home. On board the ship, they met quite a few interesting people. Colonel Riverton had been right. India did cast a spell on one. She had only spent a month and a half and yet she knew that she would miss its bright people, colours, smells and culture. She could now relate to the British ICS men and their families, who had spent decades in India and had fallen in love with the country. Many were heartbroken that they would not see her shores again. One elderly ICS man even went on to recite some poetry he had penned about the sad parting from India and as he droned on, Rachel found herself thinking with a smile – well, at least this time around, there was a poet on board!